BEAUTIFUL SINS

ENEMIES #2

PIPER LAWSON

BEAUTIFUL SINS
ENEMIES #2

"I don't know how to treat a woman like you."

I swore I'd cut Harrison King out of my life, and my bed, forever.

The second my contract with the ruthless billionaire who owned me was up...

I ran.

Not knowing that decision would only twist the web around us tighter.

Now, he's back, and the sins of his past threaten to destroy us both.

He still thirsts for power and vengeance. But his secrets run deeper than I knew.

This time, he wants me to stand by his side.

This time, he's asking.

BEAUTIFUL SINS is the steamy, enthralling continuation of Harrison and Reagan's romance that begins in *BEAUTIFUL ENEMY* and concludes in *BEAUTIFUL RUIN*.

1

RAE

*T*he cable is loose. It's fucking irritating. What kind of club doesn't have the right gear?

The kind I used to play when I was hustling to get where I am.

Where I was until last month.

This is the best of the three gigs I've played since returning to LA. The caliber of clubs I've booked has gone down since the article released featuring the photo of Harrison and me backstage at Debajo.

My renewed infamy has created a new roadblock. Now I'm not just the woman who might publicly call out a club on their bullshit.

I'm also a hypocrite.

Still, we're in LA, and this venue is full of beautiful people in various stages of intoxication.

A small film crew occupies one side. Beck's in the center, security watching him and the crew surrounding him.

The entire set, the loose cable bugs me. Every minute, I expect the music to cut out and a bunch of partiers to throw their designer vodka drinks in my face.

But hey, at least I get to do what I love.

A month after what happened with Mischa, I still get tense during the changeover, doing a scan of the crowd before I unplug and give up the stage to descend into the throng of partiers.

Tonight, there's a college-aged kid who leans too close, trying to look down the loose black shirt that's sticking to me with sweat.

A duo of guys flanks me, making God knows what symbol over my head while they snap a pic.

A young, platinum-blond woman drags her friends over. They shift from one deadly high heel to the other while she squeals.

"Girl, I'm a huge fan! Will you be at Wild Fest next year?"

I fix on a "we're all having fun here" smile I learned from Beck. "You'll have to wait and see."

"Ohmigod. It's going to be the biggest thing." She makes a duck face next to me as she wraps an arm around my shoulders. "I want life lessons from anyone who can land Harrison King. He's loaded and gorgeous and that accent... I bet he fucks like an animal."

As the flash goes off, I'm not seeing the camera or the woman.

All I can remember are the memories I've tried to shove down. Harrison King, body straining and damp with sweat, me clinging to him and gasping as he drove into me until we both collapsed.

But it was all a lie. It meant nothing.

"Dammit, one more?" the girl asks, but I'm already pushing away.

"Hey!" A whistle cuts through the noise, and I wait for Beck to catch up. "Heading out early?"

My friend is Hollywood-leading-man handsome, with dark hair and darker eyes that see more than they let on. His looks might've helped land him his primetime show, but his shrewdness got him the reality series he's filming now.

"Yeah. Thanks for bringing the crew here," I say.

The club made a few extra bucks, plus free publicity, for allowing Beck's crew to film an episode of the reality show here. If they didn't already want me back on the strength of my set, they will now.

"How many selfies did you take before someone brought your boy up?"

I shake my head. "It's been a month. He's living his life. I'm living mine." I eye his crew. "You should get back to the girl you were sucking face with. She's already bailed on her friends."

He glances back that way, where a beautiful, fresh-faced woman stands next to his security.

He goes to speak with her, then two minutes later, he's back, ushering me into the rear seat of a limo.

"Shouldn't have done that," I tell him as I drop my bag on the floor and he reaches for a bottle of champagne in the fridge.

"You're my friend." He pops the cork and pours a glass, passing it to me. "So, I heard that chick ask about Wild Fest. *Are* you mixing there?"

I stare into the champagne flute, its tiny bubbles at odds with the leaden feeling inside me. "I got on their radar this spring before everything, but they've been dodging me since Ibiza."

"That's why you're pissy? It has nothing to do with Harrison King?"

"Nothing." I take a long drink, the bubbles tickling my throat, then burning after I swallow.

I pull off the headphones still around my neck and tuck them carefully into the bag at my feet.

Beck leans over, his handsome face suddenly close.

I frown. "What are you doing?"

"Testing your claim."

He covers my mouth with his.

His lips are determined and playful at once as he kisses me.

My hands freeze in midair, too stunned to do anything else. He dares me to pull back.

I let the feeling wash over me. He's warm, masculine, compelling in a totally unselfconscious, totally Beck way.

But it's not dangerous or breathtaking. My heart rate is up from surprise, not arousal.

When his tongue parts my lips, I shove at his chest.

Beck drops back against the seat with a laugh. "See? You're still hung up on the guy."

"Just because I don't want to fuck you doesn't mean I'm hung up on someone else."

"You're kidding, right? Have you seen me?"

His words eat at the wall around my heart.

"Thanks for trying to make me feel better. Even if it was a fucked-up way to do it."

"I can't fix your heart, but I can say you have no reason to feel ashamed of what you did in Ibiza. Whatever makes you so critical started a long time ago with shit you don't think about in the light of the day, not to mention talk about."

"You get all that from me not letting you stick your tongue in my mouth?"

He shakes his head. "Been watching you a while, Little Queen. You haven't made peace with who you are. You want to play the Wild Fests of this world, you gotta do that sooner or later." His phone rings, and he mouths, "My producer," as he answers.

I drag out my own phone and pull up my social accounts.

Harrison King watch has resumed. He has left Ibiza. Since the photos of us surfaced, he's been seen in London. Paris. At his clubs, but also with women.

What surprises me most is how the pictures make my chest ache. An unrelenting ache that lingers through days of trying to work, dinners with friends, nights alone.

How I feel has nothing to do with his hard,

beautiful body or strong hands or firm lips or piercing blue eyes, and everything to do with the fact that I felt as if he showed me parts of himself he'd never shown anyone else.

Admitting what happened to his parents, that he's on a mission to redeem them. He'd do anything to win La Mer and rebuild the empire that fell when they died, the same empire I threatened when I exposed him on social media.

Anything—including using me.

I don't believe he set up the pictures of us at Debajo, but he must have seen them, and he hasn't reached out once.

Not a damn word. No defending what happened in his clubs or how it looked as if he used me.

I need to move on.

I haven't been up to New York because I know Annie will want to talk—the kind of talk with way too many feelings—and I'm avoiding getting into that.

Which is why I'm in a limo with Beck, who has not only given me a place to stay the past few weeks when I didn't want to be alone, but who should be fucking a perfectly nice girl instead of looking after me.

There's an email with a subject and sender that leap off the page.

"What's wrong?" Beck asks, and I realize he's hung up his call.

"My brother Kian's getting married in a month. He's inviting me."

"Short notice. Where's the wedding?"

"Napa." I fold my arms at his raised brow. "I grew up in Orange County."

His low rumble of laughter has me sighing. "You've been back a month, and I bet you haven't told any of them."

Shadows flick across his face from the streetlights, but it's the darkness inside me that makes me shiver.

"We haven't been close since high school."

Beck pulls my head down on his shoulder and lays his on top of mine. "Here's the thing. You could be a superstar. Have the Wild Fests of the world begging you to show. But you won't get there until you make peace with where you've been. No matter where you're going, you can't run from you."

"Have you made peace?" I ask him pointedly.

He's had trouble with his parents—they're flush and part of New York society, and from what

I understand, having their son turn his back on the career his father wanted for him to pursue acting and come out publicly as bi pushed their self-righteous buttons.

He sighs. "Work in progress."

I grab the champagne and chug the rest, then turn off my phone and shove it in my bag, leaving the top open. The glint of diamond headphones follows me home.

2

HARRISON

*I*t's not the first time I've tried to open a new door in my life—metaphorically or literally.

Nor is it the first time the way has been thoroughly barricaded.

"How long will this take?" I bark into my Bluetooth headphones, kicking at the stack of cinderblocks barring the entrance to the warehouse.

"Depends. The documents you shared about your parents weren't much to go on." The other man's Northern Irish accent abrades my ears.

"So go to other sources. You're the investigator." Cobwebs cover my hands as I lift a brick and set it a dozen feet away.

"You can't just go around asking whether dead people were involved in illicit activities."

I toss my tie over my shoulder as I bend to grab two more. "Should be easier than when they were alive."

My top priority is convincing Christian my parents were innocent so he'll sell me La Mer. Hence the investigator.

My father helped build the legitimate side of Mischa's family's business, acquiring and managing real estate and venues. I didn't think much of it until the summer after my fist year of uni in Connecticut. I arrived home to find them looking so drained even a self-indulgent nineteen-year-old would notice something was wrong.

They looked over their shoulders when we were out. Stayed in the living room, speaking in hushed tones late at night. While I had been at school, they'd become unhappy ghosts of the people who raised me.

Which was why I told them to leave the Ivanov family's business.

They were in the process of doing that when they were killed, their deaths made to look like drug overdoses.

"Someone is alleging my parents not only

knew the full nature of what transpired in that business but enabled it."

If anyone but Christian needed the kind of proof I hired the investigator to find, I'd have dismissed it as ugly conjecture. However, what Christian thinks matters because I need to buy his club in order to bury Mischa once and for all.

"You have thirty days to definitively return evidence they were innocent."

I click off more forcefully than necessary and toss the earpieces in my pocket as footsteps approach me from behind.

"Sounds juicy, boss." Leni pops a hand on a hip as I grab the last of the blocks blocking the door.

"Christian's holding out on La Mer. I thought he and my father were good friends. Turns out there was something between them. A misunderstanding, no doubt. My father was a decent man."

"And if he wasn't?"

I frown at the sun over the top of the warehouse, sweat making my shirt stick to my back. "Everything I'm doing to rebuild what they started is for them. I can't believe he would have knowingly helped build an empire on people's suffering." I grab my pocket square and wipe the dirt off my hands, the sweat at the base of my neck. "Digging up the truth is my investigator's business. In the meantime, this is ours."

She turns to survey the property. "Looks like shit."

"Most diamonds do before they're polished." I unlock the door and gesture inside. "After you."

The space is massive, a single open rectangle with concrete floors and industrial lighting suspended thirty feet up.

The floor plans I reviewed say there are offices at one end, which we can use. The dozen loading docks are overkill. We might use one, but the rest need to be closed off or redesigned.

"How long to renovate it into a nightclub?" I ask.

"Assuming the permits and zoning are lined up... a year."

"They're not, and I want it in six months."

Her laughter dies. "You're serious?"

"I'm not waiting around while Christian passes judgment. Echo will continue to expand. We've been making acquisitions, but we can't ignore development opportunities. This will be our next nightclub."

Rumors of the nightclub industry's downfall are overblown. The clubs that are closing are ones where the owners don't understand the business they're in and don't evolve to deliver their function in new ways.

A club isn't a venue that serves drinks.

It's a theme park.

A secret rendezvous.

Hell, even a runway.

It's a vehicle for thrills. The thrill made by being swept up in the darkness, the music, of watching and putting on a show.

Leni sighs. "I'll see what I can do about the timeline. Work our contractor contacts, assuming we can pay twice regular rates."

"One and a half," I correct. "I'll take care of the zoning and permits."

LA is a city built for that twisted intersection of the elegant and the hedonistic, the cultured and the primal.

This area includes some studio buildings and storage. It's close enough to Hollywood and most LA neighborhoods to get people in, and transit is established, though I expect most people will arrive by car.

Still, I've heard it's tough to get through the zoning committees. We need to show them that putting a mixed-use entertainment venue here will be an asset to the local community rather than a liability.

"Why are you even here, converting some warehouse instead of running La Mer?" Leni prods. "I thought you and Christian were working it out."

"I told him I'd prove to him I could run it and suggested an artist who could step in for the long weekend."

"And?"

"And the day after I promised that, she left."

My feet echo on the concrete as I cross the space, heading for the doors at the far side.

Leni cocks her head. "Let me guess—she doesn't know about La Mer. Because your pride stopped you from telling her or from asking her to stay."

"It's not pride. She made it clear she wants nothing more to do with me."

I grimace as I reach the door labeled OFFICE, try the handle. It gives. I peer into the darkness, feeling for a light switch. When I find it, the overhead light clicks on, showing a surprisingly decent space with furniture still in place.

This summer with Raegan was unexpected. I

might've been the one to trick her into playing Debajo, but the joke was on me.

I felt way too fucking much around her. Not only was she beautiful and talented and stubborn. I wanted to fix the damned world for her, to make myself and everything around me worthy.

None of it mattered because she left at the first opportunity.

It's unreasonable to blame her after what happened with Mischa. But I do.

I blame her.

Because whatever I felt, she didn't feel the same, or she would've stayed.

Leni passes me and drags a finger across the dusty desk. "Rae's playing in LA, you know."

My abs clench at the sound of her name.

When Rae left, I needed to get my head out of my ass and move on with my business. Part of that was being seen at events, which I squared my shoulders for and undertook. I needed to play the game and be seen playing it.

Still... Every suggestive look, every overt invitation from women in my social circle, I've turned down.

It's a strange combination, being available and

being utterly uninterested in anyone but the one person I can't have.

"You've been a bear since she left. What're you going to do about it?"

I glare. "I liked you better when you weren't up in my business."

"You're the one who hired me. Still can't quite figure out why you picked up a bunch of misfits. Me, Natalia, Toro, half the people in your business."

"My father always said to put the right people around you. I need a team that doesn't require coddling to do what has to be done."

Leni cocks a brow. "And she fits right in. Rae's tougher than I thought. I like her. And you do too, or you wouldn't have taken a sudden interest in a Burbank warehouse that's sat vacant since you bought it a year ago."

"I'm not here for her. This is business." I survey the room, imagining the dusty furniture replaced with more modern trappings.

"Let's pretend that's true. Rae's taken a hit, but her cult following is devoted. If we can get this place ready in six months, we'll need to book talent. You've gotten a lot of bad press this year but still came out on top. Mischa didn't press charges.

No patrons were hurt at Debajo the night you two decided to bring your little fight club to town. Not that I'm complaining, but next time? Give me a heads-up so I can sell tickets."

My gaze snaps to Leni's.

I knew Rae was here when I decided to move this launch up the priority list for Echo, but she wasn't the reason. I was done hiding out in Ibiza, licking my wounds, and needed to get back to running a growing corporation—one ready and able to bury Mischa's once and for all.

"Not everything comes back to her," I say.

My friend crosses to me and brushes off my suit. "So, why did you have a check printed instead of having her final payment wired to her like the others?" She taps my breast pocket. "Don't worry, Harry. If I didn't know you so well, I'd have no idea you were still obsessed with her."

***

The check burns a hole in my breast pocket.

Through my suit, my shirt.

Possibly my skin.

When a member of Echo's team reached out to see where we could deliver the check this morning, Rae responded with the address of a studio lot. They purposely didn't say I would be the one coming.

The sun bakes my neck, my face damp under my sunglasses as I approach the trailer. The door opens, and two figures emerge—a young, athletic man with a woman slung over one shoulder and a stack of papers in his other hand.

The woman's curvy legs are encased in faded skinny jeans. One flip-flop falls off her foot, landing next to the steps of the trailer.

"You owe me a shoe," she huffs.

"Call my people," Beck replies cheerfully.

"Fuck your people. I'll stage an uprising in your closet while you're sleeping. Throw one of your five-hundred-dollar loafers out the bedroom window and see how much you like that."

The familiarity of Rae's low mutter is a kick in my gut. The feelings I've been shoving down rise up at once, colliding and combusting in a way that feels uncannily like heartburn.

"Excuse me, do you have ID?" A woman shifts out of a golf cart in front of me.

"I'm Harrison King."

Before she can stop me, I round the golf cart, leaving her behind.

"Well, this I didn't expect." Beck's amused, and his insolent drawl when he spots me has my nostrils flaring.

Rae shifts on his shoulder. "What's going on?"

"We've got company." He releases her, bending to set her on the ground with a thud.

It's an easy movement, as if they do this all the time.

I fucking hate it.

Rae straightens her top as she squares to face me.

She's the same as I remember... and different. Slow curves even understated clothes can't hide. Dark hair tumbling over her shoulders, eyes framed with thick lashes narrowed in my direction so I can't read the emotion beneath even if I want to.

And I want to. I'd give every dollar in my damn wallet to know what's going through her head when we look at each other for the first time in a month.

It's been thirty-two days, actually, since I left her in my room in Ibiza.

That night, I wanted to stay with her but forced myself to carry out my duties as owner of Debajo and as a King. I went to see the police, then Christian.

Beck holds up the sheaf of papers. "I'm gonna go read. You need anything, I'm on lunch for another thirty."

She nods as he walks away.

Of the things I've pictured her doing since she left me, Beck wasn't one of them. Jealousy is a living thing in my chest as I consider what they were doing in that trailer together.

The possibility that he gets to touch her, gets to see her smile, gets to fucking *make* her smile...

It's agony.

Rae closes the distance, grabbing my jacket and tugging me to the side of the trailer as a golf cart flies by.

"What are you doing here?" she asks.

I drag my sunglasses off, tucking them into the pocket of my suit. What am I doing here? If I had a reason, it's lost in her eyes.

That's when I remember the envelope. "I was in LA for business and wanted to drop this off."

Rae's brows pull together as she accepts the envelope, opens it, and sucks in a breath. "This is more than my cut."

"We filled Debajo, which exceeded even my expectations. You deserve it."

Dark, troubled eyes search mine.

"Besides," I go on, impulsive, "I wasn't sure where to send the espresso machine, and you wouldn't use it anyway."

Rae shoves a hand through her hair, looking as if she can't decide whether to laugh or scream.

I want her to say she made a mistake by leaving. That she still thinks of me late at night after her shows.

Instead, Rae lifts the edge of my suit and tucks the envelope back in my pocket over my heart, her gaze lingering on my shirt as if she can see the scar beneath. "You don't owe me anything."

But it's the look she gives me before turning and starting back toward the trailer door—not angry but sad, overwhelmed—that steels me.

"You owe me something." She stops, and I press on. "You left my bed without saying goodbye."

Rae turns slowly. "You didn't see the article?"

"I saw it. That's what happens when you're in the public eye. You grow a thick skin because the arrows only get sharper."

Her voice rises, her hands fisting at her sides. "I

woke up to that news story, to the world calling me a hypocrite and someone I cared about shoving it in my face."

"Are you a hypocrite?"

"I don't know!" she retorts. "You didn't come back all night. I tried calling you. Waited for hours."

Each word is a knife in my gut.

I figured she'd decided I wasn't worth sticking around for, like everything else in her life. I wasn't going to reach out to her and beg her to reconsider.

The possibility she'd taken the article to heart never occurred to me.

She's so fucking young right now. It should be a warning, another brick in a fortress of reasons I can't have her, but all I want to do is drag her against me.

"You tried to reach me when I was at the police station," I say, clenching my hands into fists so I don't touch her. "I stopped to see Christian on the way home. When I got back, you'd left."

Raegan doesn't blink. "What about the issues with the clubs?"

"I swear I cleaned house. I told you I would

make them better, and I did. There've been no issues since. Not a single claim."

She wants to believe me. I want her to, though I have no right to ask.

"The article made me question a lot of things," she says at last. "Things I'd stopped questioning while I was in Ibiza, playing for a man who was my enemy. One I swore I'd never support again."

"He's grateful."

Her eyes cloud, either at the expression on my face or the humility in my voice.

I won't beg. But seeing her like this, knowing where she's coming from, I need to make her understand.

I can live with being a villain, but I won't let her be one.

"I have somewhere to be," she says.

"I'll walk you out."

She reaches into the trailer, coming back with the same backpack she toted around Ibiza. The top is open, and I catch a glimpse of the contents before she flips the top closed.

"He can't do what I can do, " I say as we fall into step next to each other and head down the road between studios, runners and golf carts passing every minute.

"I'll be the judge of that."

The clawing in my chest has my hands clenching into fists.

Hello, jealousy. It's been a while.

"Tell me you're not fucking him." I laugh, but underneath, I'm livid.

"That is every shade of not your business."

"It is because you still have feelings for me."

Rae pulls up, looking indignant.

"You kept the headphones I gave you."

She follows my gaze to the now-closed bag on her back, where I'd caught a glimpse of them in the sunlight. "They're diamond."

"And you live out of a single bag. You wouldn't want the reminder staring at you every day. So, if you were over what happened between us, you would've pawned them without blinking, love."

The endearment slips out, but I hide my surprise. She can't mask hers, though, and it's worth the mistake for the way she swallows hard.

When I talked with Leni, I was still telling myself I could move past Rae. Now, I realize...

I don't want to.

I resume my ambling toward the road until she catches up to me, her fingers digging into my skin through the jacket. This might be the first time I've wished I was wearing a polo shirt instead of a suit, if only to feel her touch without asking for it.

"What are you doing here, Harrison?" she demands. "You think you can keep an eye on me?"

"I purchased a lot in Burbank. It's an industrial warehouse I've been planning to convert to an entertainment venue."

"You're opening a new club."

"I need an act opening night. And whether you get off on my cock or just thinking about it"—her dark eyes flash—"you still owe me two favors."

"Not legally enforceable." Her voice is full of disbelief.

"But you're not a woman who goes back on your commitments. It's why you don't make them lightly. When you're done arguing with yourself, you know where to reach me."

I savor her stunned expression as I press the envelope into her palm.

It's hardly enough to tide me over until she comes back, but it'll have to do.

3

RAE

"*N*o way that's going to happen. We need staff on those hours," says Callie as she rounds the corner to her cubicle and pulls up when she spots me.

"We'll catch up later," she says to the phone, clicking off. Her outfit is tidy business casual, a threadbare blue skirt and knit white T-shirt with nude sandals.

"Greetings." I lift a hand.

Since returning from Ibiza, I've only had a couple of texts from my cousin in response to mine, and I'm done with it.

That's why I'm showing up in person at the small office in a strip mall that houses the charity where she works.

"You can't stay. I have a meeting in ten minutes." She glances around the room as if she's looking for a door to eject me from.

"We've both been there for one another over the years. On some serious shit," I emphasize. "So don't go hating on me all of a sudden."

Her expression clouds, and I know she's thinking of our shared past.

"Come on, Callie. You don't actually think I was having some affair with a man I thought was bad news?"

She tucks her dark hair behind her ear and sighs. "I think you might've gotten caught up in what he was selling. You did lie to me about who you were with. I don't want to see you get hurt again."

It's true that I lied. But Harrison showed up yesterday and rocked me—not with the check, but with his words.

He's not in LA for me, but fuck... it felt like it.

"I got carried away," I admit.

Callie cocks her head, lowers her voice so no one outside can hear. "On some level, I get it. He's pretty extra, Rae. An actual billionaire? He's nothing like the guys we went to high school with."

"Because they were such princes," I remind her.

Her shoulders slump. "Fair enough. They were all assholes back then. The guys and the girls."

My chest tightens at the unwanted memories that rise up. The rejection from the people who claimed to have my back. The isolation of feeling as if no one else I knew was going through the same thing.

It wasn't Harrison's money or status that seduced me. It was the way he wanted me, the way he made me feel more than myself. In Ibiza, at Debajo, I started to believe I was part of something again.

The shock of Mischa's appearance and the article the next morning about me and Harrison reminded me I'd slipped into that dependence without noticing.

A woman sticks her head in the doorway with an apologetic look. "Callie, you need to be out of here in half an hour. Even if you'd work all the hours for free, Ramona needs the office."

"Who's Ramona?" I demand as the woman leaves again.

"The money you sent helped—it helped a lot, and we'll pay you back. In the meantime, we gave up a couple of offices to another organization to save money."

I look out into the hall to see women filling a waiting room, some reading, some staring at the floor. Another is pacing the floor, her dark hair swinging in a long ponytail that reaches her belt.

"I can get you more money," I tell Callie.

She folds her arms. "No. You've already given us more than enough."

I think of the check from Harrison.

What affected me more than the gesture was his words. The fact that he thinks I'm still into him.

It's crap, of course.

But with his blue eyes staring into me, it was hard not to feel something...

Still, even if he's here, I can't just forget every-thing that went down. Callie's right that I got caught up in his world. We're back on my turf, and it won't happen again.

"I RSVPed for Kian's wedding."

My cousin's words jar me out of my head.

"He invited me too. I'm thinking of going."

Her brows shoot up. "Really? That would be...big."

My stomach knots and I shove my hands in my pockets, thinking of Beck's comments the other night. "Do you think we have to make peace with the past to move forward with our lives?"

"Peace seems ambitious. But I do know that arguing with things that have already happened only brings us more pain." Callie's gaze flicks toward the hall. "A lot of the women who come through these doors think they're broken in some way. They're looking for justice, or vindication, or absolution. But often what they really need is to know that they get to choose how to act, how to feel, who they want to be today. That's all any of us can control."

BLUE is darker than its namesake color. A black club with fish tanks around the perimeter.

I haven't been here since the week before Tyler and Annie's wedding when I played and saw a woman assaulted.

Harrison promised he fixed the problems at this club, and the others.

I need to know if he's telling the truth.

I put on high heels and a short, black dress and plum lipstick. There's mace in my bag, though it's more of a security blanket than anything.

Inside, I head to the bar alone.

This place is a shark tank, but I'm not the bait. Instead I scan the crowd, looking for men doing the same kind of looking I am. Searching for a particular kind of partner.

The DJ is good, a guy I've heard locally and in New York. But I'm not here for the music tonight.

"Can I buy you a drink?"

A tall guy with dark hair and a leering grin cuts off my view of the dance floor.

"I'm a big girl, I can get my own."

"Baby, you shouldn't have to."

Ignoring my rejection, he reaches a hand around my waist to grab my ass.

I shove at him. "I said I'm not interested."

"Sure you are. We're getting along great." He tries again, and this time I shove harder, stepping back, bodies bumping mine in the dense crowd.

"Excuse me. Is he bothering you?"

My heart pounds as I look up to see security at my shoulder.

"No," the guy snorts, annoyed.

"Yes," I say at the same time.

The security guy moves between us. "We have a zero-tolerance policy for harrassment. That means you have to leave."

The guy puts up a protest, but security escorts him to the door.

A breath trembles out of me. This time when I scan the room, I spot security at several points around the perimeter. They're attentive. Focused. On the crowd *and* the DJ booth.

Tonight could be an anomaly. But judging by the robust staff, this isn't the same club it was.

"Yes?" the bartender shouts over the music, and I reluctantly turn to face her.

"Whisky. Neat." She reaches for a bottle, and I lean over the counter. "Wait."

I see Harrison's fingerprints all over this place, and I want to believe he meant it when he said he changed things here.

"Glen Scotia. Thirty-year-old."

She stares at me long enough I think I spoke Greek. But finally, she bends under the bar and retrieves a bottle.

"It's two hundred," she says as she pours.

"I'm celebrating."

"Anything in particular?"

"Faith in mankind."

I click into my messages and fire off a text.

Harrison King might not be finished with me, but we're in my territory now.

I can handle myself. For a moment in Ibiza, I questioned it, and that was my mistake. Not trusting him, but failing to trust myself.

Rae: I have a DJ who might work for your opening. But she's expensive.

My phone rings, and I answer, straining to hear over the music.

"Expensive is my favorite price."

God, he's arrogant. The British accent only makes him sound more elitist. But damn if I don't love the sound of his voice over the line.

"You want me working for you again?"

"I enjoy you under me. I think of little else."

Heat blazes down my spine, settling into an ache knowing he replays our too-short night together as much as I do.

"Meet me tomorrow," he says. "I'll send you directions."

4

RAE

*M*y GPS announces I've arrived, but the single nondescript rectangular building on my right makes me frown. It's not a club—it's a warehouse, and I'm already regretting agreeing to meet.

The building is massive, and I park in the lot next to a row of construction vehicles and turn to the mutt in the passenger seat. "Let's go, Ernie."

I round to the passenger side and lift Beck's pet out of the car, careful of the stitches from his surgery.

"For a dog, you've got the princess act down," I comment as I set him on the pavement, fastening his leash as he cocks his head up at me.

We head for the door nearest the parking lot,

which is propped open with a two by four. The moment I enter, I'm astounded by the sheer size of the place.

"What do you think?" Leni calls from the other end.

"It looks like an empty Target," I point out as she approaches.

Two dozen workers are bustling, alone and in groups, many on ladders and scaffolding.

"Try telling *him* that. We're insulating the walls," Leni supplies. "Floors are next. Anything we can upgrade as a 'warehouse'"—she makes air quotes—"until we get the rezoning approved."

I stop halfway across the huge room, and she bends to scratch the dog on the head.

"New man. You traded up."

"I can hear you," comes an irritated British voice.

I straighten as Harrison makes his way across the floor, his dark suit fitting his form to perfection.

The little tremor starts in my stomach, spreads lower into a tingling between my thighs and up to my breasts. I'm a teenager thinking dirty thoughts about the bad boy in school. The older one who's the kind of trouble you'd risk everything for.

Since Ibiza, the memories faded a little every week, until I could get through almost a day without remembering his scent, his presence, the way he looked at me as if I were a piece of fine art.

Now, it's roaring back.

"Oh good. I thought I might have to speak louder," Leni responds as he stops in front of us.

"Don't you have a job to do?" Harrison gripes.

"Sure, boss." She winks before offering me a fist bump. "Good to see you. We need to go surfing sometime. Girls' day."

The next moment, she's gone and it's Harrison and me. We might be surrounded by construction workers, but the pull between us is electric.

My attention drags over every perfectly tailored inch of him. "What would it take for you to ditch the suit? Global wool shortage? Zombie apocalypse? Male menopause?"

"I'm pleased to hear your interest in getting me out of my clothes hasn't waned." Warmth dances in his eyes, and I feel it everywhere. It's impossible not to respond to this man.

"I said I'd talk about opening a club. Which, by the way, this is far from."

"Good thing I have a talent for seeing what things could be."

Is he still talking about the club?

"There need to be lines." I nod toward the tape on the floor.

"Some boundaries are legitimate. Others are notional, have zero grounding in reality, and are simply erected to protect things not worth protecting." He crosses the line of tape without a second look. "I won't play by made-up rules. Yours or anyone else's."

Those lashes are a mile long, and I'm caught between staring at them and his firm mouth.

"What's with the dog?"

I jerk back, realizing he was looking at my feet.

"Ernie's Beck's. He had surgery, and I didn't want to put a cone on him. Beck has a busy day at the studio, and E doesn't like hanging out in the trailer, plus the PAs don't have time."

"You're living with Beck." His gaze sharpens.

"Careful. I'll put a cone on you."

Harrison leans in. "I'd like to see you try."

If I told myself I'd exaggerated the power of what was between us in Ibiza, I was wrong. He might not be the happy-ever-after kind, but Harrison King and I have a boatload of chemistry.

A forty-five-meter yacht's worth and then some.

"So, according to Leni, you're praying this behemoth will be a club?"

He folds his arms. "In six months," he confirms. "And there's no prayer involved."

"Really? Because when my brother, Kian, built his medical practice from scratch, there was a shit ton of zoning and permitting and paperwork, none of which is easy here, where 'not-in-my-backyard syndrome' is elevated from a pastime to a full-on passion."

His eyes darken dangerously, and I raise a brow.

"I never knew you were acquainted with real estate development. It's distractingly sexy."

"Then stay focused. This is going to be the dance floor?" I motion to the center of the space. "What about bars?"

"On either side. Come to my office. I'll show you the drawings."

"It's better out here."

Harrison's slow grin is devastating. "You don't trust yourself alone with me."

"I don't trust you."

But I need more than his word that this place will be performance-ready in six months. So, I follow him.

"You think I'm sufficiently base," he murmurs as I fall into step beside him, "that while you're looking at floor plans, I'll reach over and unfasten the button on those jeans. Peel them down your legs but leave them on your ankles when I lift you onto the desk because the idea of you being trapped turns me on."

His words might as well be stroking up my inseam, rubbing against my clit at the top, for the way they affect me.

He pauses outside the door, angling his aristocratic profile toward me. "Or do you think I'll find out if you're wearing the lingerie you bought to wear for me on your birthday?"

He's smug, but the way he grips the door handle, as if all of this matters more than he's letting on, makes me ache.

"I didn't buy it for you."

"You bought it to see if you could bring me to my knees," he corrects. "Be careful what you wish for. You might enjoy the view."

He holds the door, and when I finally brush past him, I'm still thinking of him that night after Debajo, how breathtaking it was to have him over me and inside me, dragging us both over a cliff to a fate neither of us wanted to escape.

How much more devastating could he be from his knees?

His control is one thing. His reverence would be another.

I understand he had reasons for not being available the morning after he left me, but that doesn't mean I'll fall into bed with him now. Neither will I give up who I am or what I want to get caught up in his world.

The office is spacious, a large L-shaped desk facing the door and a coffee table with a low gray sofa and two plush-looking chairs in one corner. Behind the door sits a row of filing cabinets. It's a mashup of used minimalist pieces and opulence.

He doesn't seem uncomfortable with the contrast.

"I'm surprised at your persistence," I comment.

He leaves the door ajar, possibly to make me more comfortable.

Or to prove that whatever's going to happen between us won't be derailed by a dozen contractors.

"At recruiting a DJ?"

"At recruiting me." I select the chair nearest the door and sink into it, lifting Ernie into my lap —possibly to use as a canine shield. "There are plenty of people you could hire with less baggage."

"You've repeatedly told me you only have one bag. And still you manage to lose it."

I ignore the tug in my chest at his familiar teasing. "Is this about sex? Because if you think what happened between us the last night in Ibiza is enough to make me fall back into bed with you, you're wrong."

"If it was only about sex, I'd have you on your back right now."

He's utterly confident he's right. But if it's not about sex for him, what's left?

"You were engaged once," I say. "It ended badly. I have a hard time believing you're here to sweep me off my feet."

Harrison rummages through a stack of papers on his desk, tugging at the knot on his tie. When he crosses to me, laying blueprints out on the coffee table and claiming the next chair, I can't help inhaling his scent.

"There's a fascinating mile between you screaming my name and me on my knee with a box, love."

Those soul-stealing blue eyes bore into me.

What would it take for Harrison King to put his

scars and suspicions behind him and open his heart, his life, to a woman?

I reach across Ernie to tug the papers toward me, but Harrison doesn't release the blueprints, and our fingers brush, heat zinging through me.

His thighs clench under the expensive fabric of his pants, and his exhale is half groan.

All I hear is the hammering of my pulse. Harrison's smoldering gaze burns me up from the inside.

Our faces are inches apart, his firm lips parted. "La Mer isn't yet mine, but with this in my collection of venues, I'll surpass Mischa in growth. With or without La Mer."

I turn my attention back to the blueprints, scanning the scale drawings that include the bars, the lighting, the stage.

They're impressive.

"So, I'm supposed to believe you'll get everything done on schedule because Harrison King wills it so?"

"Because you know what I'm capable of."

It's what makes him a powerful ally, and a dangerous one.

"If you can get your approvals lined up and show me this place is coming together, I'll sign on. For this amount." I reach for the pen in his jacket pocket, pull his hand toward me, and scrawl a number on his palm as he watches, bemused.

"You're joking."

"My rate's gone up since Ibiza."

My rate for him has, anyway.

Harrison stares at me incredulously. Every inch of his perfect body is tense, and he's not bothering to hide the impatience on his face. "Are you forgetting I *made* you in Ibiza?"

"Actually, I made *you*. The Debajo door doubled under me."

"And you trembled under me."

Before I can respond, he jerks me toward him.

His lips claim mine, hot and possessive.

There's no questioning in this kiss. It's punishment and regret, a dark cocktail crafted by his hard mouth and demanding tongue.

I try not to respond. His grip on my hair is demanding, but I can't bring myself to pull away.

I've been fantasizing about kissing him for an entire month, afraid it would never happen again. Now that it's happening, that low throb in my body starting up like it never stopped, I remember why.

Ernie whines in my lap, but Harrison doesn't

relent until he's tasted me to his satisfaction, until I'm panting and my heart is racing against my ribs.

When he pulls back, his arrogant face is clouded with desire.

"You don't have the right to do that," I manage.

"I never had the right. Wasn't a problem before." He rubs a hand across his hard jaw, eyes dancing. "And don't pretend you didn't enjoy it."

I want to slap him.

I want him to press me down on this coffee table and see if it'll hold both our weights.

Before I can decide, his phone buzzes and he glances at it. "I have a meeting tomorrow with the man in charge of zoning. We've gotten permits to upgrade the walls, flooring, anything that wouldn't raise suspicions for warehouse use. The rest will have to wait until the zoning is completed. In the interim, I've had my marketing team mock-up some options for promoting opening night. I want to go over plans with you. Tomorrow night, over dinner."

"We could meet for a drink after dinner. I have dinner plans."

He frowns. "With?"

"None of your business. Drinks after," I repeat. His eyes flash as I rise to stand.

He walks me to the door of the building, Ernie trotting at our heels.

"It's a date," Harrison calls.

"It's drinks, asshole."

His slow grin is smug, as if our banter gives him divine pleasure he's been denied for too long. With a look that steals my breath, he turns and heads back inside

My fingers tighten on Ernie's leash, and as I head across the parking lot, I call Harrison King every filthy name I know.

RAE

"Come on, baby. Give it to me," I mutter.

"All you had to do was ask."

I glance over my shoulder as Beck enters the kitchen in shorts and nothing else.

"Your coffee maker's acting up." The gleaming silver machine is the same brand Harrison bought in Ibiza.

"When sweet talk fails..." He bangs a hand on the side. "Try now."

I do, and it runs. "Huh."

He winks. "That's what I'm here for."

"I decided to go to Kian's wedding. Maybe I can put the past behind me."

"Need a plus one?"

"Nope. I'm not inviting anyone into that cesspool."

"Rae, there's a lot of ugly in this world. You can't handle your own family, maybe you're not ready for it."

I fold my arms. "Nothing ever happened to you in your past that you wouldn't want to revisit, or have dragged out, or have connected to who you are now?"

He frowns. "I'm not hiding anything. Are you?"

Steam erupts from the coffee machine, and I attend to it. My stomach knots, and I force myself to keep breathing. "I'd rather think about my future."

"Wouldn't we all." Beck barks out a laugh as he grabs a mug from the cabinet.

The huge silver fridge is stocked with healthy prepped foods. Beck won't let me contribute to the mortgage, but I hacked his grocery delivery account and switched it to my credit card.

When I first met Beck through Annie in college, I never could've predicted I'd be staying with him now, sharing coffee, not to mention a roof.

Beck's good at making friends and keeping them. I'm suspicious of everyone's motives, waiting for them to bail, but he's the opposite—he expects the best and often finds it. He has a knack for seeing through someone's defenses to what's underneath. But unlike many, he doesn't use it against people.

That's probably why I find myself letting him in a bit at a time and why he's often my go-to hangout partner.

Beck's phone buzzes, and he grabs it, reading the notification with a grin.

"Who's making you smile like that?"

"Emily. Chick from the club the other night."

"You can bail on our dinner plans if you want to take her out," I offer.

He slaps a hand on the counter hard enough Ernie jumps. "No way. I'm taking you for dinner tonight. A nice one. As a thanks for sitting Ernie yesterday."

The dog perks up from his designer doghouse across the kitchen.

I lean a hip against the counter. "He only tried to eat his stitches twice. I took him to see Harrison's new project."

"How is the chairman of the British Billionaire Club?" Beck asks, mischief glinting in his dark eyes as he flips his hair out of his face. "It was delightful seeing him on set. Too bad I couldn't stick around and pick ice slivers out of my chest. You know, from all those daggers shooting from his eyes."

"It wasn't that bad."

He crosses to a brown paper back next to the fridge and pulls out a pre-cut bagel before popping it into the toaster. "Dude was ready to whip it out and piss a circle around you. What'd he want?"

"To give me a bonus for Ibiza," I say as I grab the cream.

"For your legitimate, fully clothed work there," he drawls as he presses the toaster lever down.

"What are you saying?"

He turns back to me, folding his arms. "Just that he's pussy whipped. You left the boy wanting more."

I set the cream on the counter harder than necessary. "I'm not the woman who leaves guys wanting more, Beck. I'm the one who flies under the radar—unless she's on stage in a costume—and I like it that way."

"Some people are so blinded by the sun they miss the stars. Someone gets a good look at you, they're gonna find something to like."

"Wow. I was going to offer you cheese with that

bagel, but you brought your own." But my chest twinges anyway.

"So, are you gonna give him another chance?"

"To what. Irritate me? I'm already playing shitty clubs from the last time I let him in."

"Maybe he wants to make it right." The bagel pops up, and Beck reaches for a plate.

"He's turning a warehouse into a club. It's bold," I admit.

"Mmm. Bold new venture for the hotter, more insolent James Bond who wants nothing more than my girl at his exquisitely tailored side."

I roll my eyes. The man is a business titan. He has money to burn, and he didn't get that way by taking detours chasing skirts.

It's possible there's something to be learned from that.

"I'm not giving in to him. But I'm a little envious," I realize. "I think I want a warehouse."

"A warehouse," he echoes.

"Not an actual warehouse. A project I can go after no matter what. Something that's mine, that no one can say Harrison had a hand in."

My phone buzzes with a notification from Wild Fest announcing a new DJ.

"This is it." I hold up the phone, excitement surging through me. "Wild Fest. My warehouse."

"How're you going to get it? You said they're not returning your calls."

I square my shoulders. "I'll figure it out."

6

HARRISON

"*H*ope the construction outside didn't give you too much trouble. They've been working on that intersection forever. I'm Zack."

"Harrison."

The kid who heads up the zoning department for this part of LA shakes my hand. He's probably thirty, clean-cut, smells like ambition and family money. I don't need to look inside his head to know for him this is a stop on the way to something bigger.

Mayor. Governor. Maybe senator.

"I understand you're looking to develop a property in Burbank."

"It should've been zoned commercial. Everything around it is. I trust it will be straightforward after the hearing to approve the request so we can move forward with construction."

"Unfortunately, our hearing process has been delayed. We need to move yours back six weeks."

Unacceptable.

The delay will put me behind Mischa's expansion and cost me money. Every damn day this building sits empty costs money.

"This is a priority. I have significant stakes riding on finishing this on time."

He jams his hands in his pockets, eyes crinkling at the corners.

It's not a smile—it's a warning.

"I don't know how fast things move in the UK, but there can be hang-ups in California and the planning office has limited resources. We advise developers to anticipate sufficient time for approvals."

Fucker.

He's one of those types. The ones who hear I'm coming and want to make my life hell.

"If it's resources you're short, I'm sure we can expedite things."

"Just because you have money doesn't make it fast."

The rest of the meeting goes about the same, and by the time I leave, I'm in a bad mood. I slam a fist into the brick outside before heading to my car.

This new venue is my best investment to grow my company until I can clear my parents' names and convince Christian to sell me La Mer.

The entire drive back to my penthouse condo in one of LA's best hotels, I'm clenching the steering wheel.

I toss the keys to the valet and head up to my condo.

I bought the suite three years ago. Its stunning skyline and modern décor are lost on me as I toss my tie on a chair and strip down, heading for the shower.

The water makes my agitation worse.

Is it possible I was off my game?

More than once today, I've caught myself thinking of Raegan's mouth.

How I'd like to taste her everywhere else.

Whom she's going to dinner with.

When I get out and towel off, there's a buzzing in the back of my brain I can't ignore. I grab my phone and check Beck's social media.

Good food, better company.

The image shows Beck grinning, his arm

around a woman with her hand in front of her face. But her amused smile is visible and, for me, recognizable.

My abs clench.

When she said she had a dinner she couldn't change, I assumed she meant it was something important.

Unless he's more important to her than me.

The napkins on the table, deep plum, edge into the frame. I stalk to the kitchen and yank open the top drawer to find the same napkins.

But I can't get over the way she's smiling in the picture. I can't remember making her smile like that.

On impulse, I veer away from the closet full of designer suits.

Instead, I choose trousers and a gray shirt, fasten the cuffs.

Top button?

I undo it.

Better.

I take the elevator downstairs and head for the restaurant.

It's full of stunning couples and small groups. It's one couple I'm looking for. I don't see her, but I spot his dark head.

I catch sight of myself in the mirror. The casual shirt can't hide the agitation beneath the surface.

Cutting the maître d' a look that brooks no argument, I head back to the table.

"We're good on wine, thank... you." Beck's brows lift as I sink into the chair across from him.

"You're the dinner date."

He spreads his hands. "Guilty as charged."

My gaze runs over the tablecloth. They've eaten their entrees, and a single dessert menu rests between the two place settings.

"We're sharing," he drawls at my look.

I came down to see her, but I want to hit him. "You're not going to keep her."

Beck cuts a look behind him before leaning an elbow along the back of his chair. "She's not a tea set. You might be a king in London, but this is LA, my friend."

I take him in, dragging my gaze slowly from his white sneakers to his designer jeans to his button-down and too-long dark hair. "We're not friends. But you don't want to be my enemy."

He leans closer. "Rae's my girl, and I don't need to fuck her to prove it. I will, however, ask the waiter to hold my phone while I use a butter knife to cut your limbs off and stuff them in any available orifice if you hurt her."

I'm still reappraising the man when Rae's startled voice cuts the tension.

"What the hell is going on?"

She's beautiful. Even the dark shadows around her eyes that I want to erase. The dress is orange, the color of the one she wore to Christian's gala, only shorter. It's as casual as the other was formal, with a scooped neck and a hem that ends halfway down her thighs.

"I decided to pick you up rather than meeting you at the club. Simple, seeing as you're eating at my hotel."

Wariness edges into her expression. "You're staying here?"

"I own the penthouse."

Rae's attention doesn't budge from me, but Beck chuckles behind his napkin. "There's an easy way to settle this." Now we both look at him. "Join us for dessert."

The waitress is at my side in an instant, eyes widening in recognition. "Mr. King. I'll bring you a whisky."

"And a chocolate mousse. Three spoons," Beck drawls.

She disappears.

"Rae and I were just discussing her next move," our smug host says.

She shoots him a warning look.

"She's opening my new club," I say.

"This is bigger. Wild Fest."

"Red Rocks amphitheater in Colorado," Rae says, shifting in her seat. "Massive outdoor event, record-breaking despite being in its third season."

"Fourth season," I correct.

"You've heard of it?"

"Of course I've heard of it."

"We're still figuring out her audition tape," Beck says.

My brows lift. "They want an actual tape?"

"Beck's talking metaphorically. It's competitive."

It's rational she would focus on a prize like that, but I'm still irritated she's spending her evening brainstorming with Beck while I was off my game because I couldn't clear my head of her.

The waitress returns with my whisky, plus dessert. Beck reaches for a spoon and dives in with an appreciative wink for the waitress, which has her flushing as she leaves.

Is this what Rae is into? Some Hollywood wannabe who's my brother's age?

She's not the woman I thought she was.

"How was your day, Harry?" Beck asks.

I ignore the nickname and swirl my drink before taking a sip. "I was preoccupied by a problem I need to resolve."

The problem being the woman in front of me.

I shift in my chair, and my knee brushes Rae's.

She jerks in her seat and her spoon clatters off her plate, falling to the carpet.

"Beck, would you excuse us?" Rae says tightly when she straightens from picking up her utensil.

Beck looks between us in amusement.

"You know, this has been fun." He rises and rounds to hug Raegan, who tries to glare at him.

"Let me get you another spoon," I say when he's gone.

I shift out of my seat to seek out new cutlery, heading toward the kitchen. I overhear our waitress talking with another whose voice I recognize. She's served me before, and I try to recall her name.

"I wasn't planning on the double shift, but when someone calls in sick, you have to," she says quietly to the other waitress. "Now I'm not sure I have time to walk home before my kid gets back from his dad's, but I can't afford to take a car."

Melanie. Madison. Mary...

"Maria," I say.

"Mr. King." She straightens, flushing. "I'm so sorry if we were too loud."

"Not at all." I order a town car while she watches, slack-jawed. "It'll be here in five minutes," I say when I hang up. "Take it wherever you need. The charges are on my account. Could I get a spoon?"

She runs to grab one, murmuring thanks as she passes it to me.

I shift back into my seat and hold out the spoon to Rae. She takes it, her gaze holding mine long enough that I wonder if she overheard the exchange.

"We have unfinished business."

"And it couldn't wait."

"No."

Rae shifts back in her seat, scanning the room behind me.

I see her shut down, feel it in her body language. It pisses me off that she can pull away emotionally while she's still within reach.

I like to come across as in control because I've

had to, which only highlights how painfully ill-equipped I am to deal with *her*.

There's no reason for me to feel out of place in this restaurant full of attractive Angelenos in their West Coast business casual. But I do. It took everything in me to walk out the door without a jacket.

And I did it for Raegan.

"I'm trying to help both of us, but you're making it exceedingly difficult," I state.

Now I have her attention. She leans in, eyes flashing as if she can burn me from the inside out. "Really? Because so far, every time I'm near you, I get holes shot in my reputation and my career. You don't get to show up here and demand I follow your rules. There's no contract this time. Who do you think you are?"

I pick up my drink and drain it. "A man who keeps asking why the fuck he bothers."

She rises from her seat and she stares at me with eyes full of fire. "Then stop."

Before Raegan reaches the door, I'm on my feet.

7

RAE

I'm over the games.

Harrison King might get any woman he wants, but he's not getting me.

I shouldn't have opened the door enough to give him a chance, but I wanted to talk about the gig. And maybe to see him. But he behaved like an utter prick, crashing my dinner with Beck like a jealous boyfriend, then acting as though I'd fucked up.

Just because he helped one of the waitstaff when he thought I couldn't hear doesn't mean he's not the devil.

I'm nearly at the front doors of the hotel when someone grabs me and tugs me behind a huge potted plant. My shoulder hits the wall. "What the fuck?"

Then he's pinning me in place with his fierce expression, filled with anger and desperation.

"You want *me* to stop?" he demands, his voice dripping with incredulity. "You came into my club, my house, my island, and turned them upside down." Harrison angles his body to box mine in, and his fingers find the nape of my neck, squeezing hard enough it steals my breath. "You fucked me like you needed it, and the next morning, you were gone. So at least be honest about your reasons. It wasn't because of some paparazzi shot. It was because you didn't believe in me enough to stay."

He's breathing as if he's been running. His corded throat is bobbing, that firm mouth parted, those piercing blue eyes full of shock and desire.

The accusation in his tone doesn't affect me, but the hurt beneath does. The rawness of his words is a reminder he was left before by a woman he trusted. I didn't leave him for another man, but his betrayed expression makes it seem as if I might as well have.

I lift my chin to meet his gaze. "What did we have? What *could* we have had, Harrison?" I swallow hard. "You were this arrogant, untouchable god, and I was this angry girl who wanted no part of your world. At least... I didn't at first."

His nostrils flare as he searches my face.

I'm playing a dangerous game, showing vulnerability to a man who crushes his, who succeeds by exploiting weakness in others. Except the throbbing low in my gut wants to believe he's not unaffected either.

"If I look like a god right now, you need reading glasses more than I do."

His self-deprecating comment makes me suck in a breath.

My attention drifts down to his open collar, the rolled-up sleeves revealing muscled forearms. I pop his collar, trailing a finger along the edge. "You're missing your suit."

He's a warrior without his armor, and I'm aching to know what convinced him to lay it down tonight.

Before I can ask, his mouth crashes down on mine.

His tongue presses at the seam of my lips, demanding entrance. I grant it to him, my body responding before my brain gives permission.

He tastes like whisky and man and I'm drowning in him.

My palms flatten against his chest to steady myself.

The rational part of me screams to get away.

Instead, I press up on my toes to kiss him back.

His arms band around me like steel.

"Too public." His muttered words cut through my haze of arousal.

Harrison doesn't take my hand but steers me across the foyer and toward a private elevator using only the force of his presence.

We step inside, and the doors shut.

His gaze is loaded with hunger, and I revel in it before he drags me up to him. Those wicked lips land on mine before sliding lower to my jaw, my neck, tracing down to my cleavage. I fist a hand in his shirt.

"Fuck." My fingers tighten in his hair as his mouth moves to cover my breast through the fabric, licking its hardened peak.

He's a storm intent on killing me and making me grateful for the mercy.

The elevator dings, and he guides me out, a firm hand on my back as we step into the huge living room of a suite.

"You never do anything halfway, do you?" I pant.

"What I want, I get." Harrison pulls back to study me, his eyes nearly black with desire. "I want you to repeat every smartass thing you've ever said to me while you're laying over my knee. I want to ride you bare before your show. To come inside you and watch you go out and play in front of a thousand people and know I'm still there. Where they all want to be. I want to tie you to my bed and make you come until you're begging me to stop."

His words seduce me. "Too many orgasms doesn't sound like a thing."

"Sweet, naïve girl."

He grips my face, his expression turning serious as he stops either of us from taking things further.

"There was one thing I wanted in my life. But since you crashed into it, I want you. Seeing you with Beck makes me crazy."

Thrilling. It's thrilling to hear him talk like this.

"How crazy?"

My lips curve, because what's crazy is the fact that this billionaire wants me, a girl with no permanent address and a closet full of damage. Harrison's shoulders pull tight under the shirt. He's gorgeous and a little reckless, his hair sticking up as if he's been running his fingers through it.

"Crazy enough I only wore a damn shirt to dinner."

I slide a hand under the edge of that shirt and rest my palm over the scars on his chest. My thumb traces the edge, and I get off on the way his pulse skips beneath my touch. "It's a good shirt," I whisper.

Riding a wave of arousal, I reach back for the knot on my dress and unfasten it. It falls to the floor.

Harrison's gaze roams my body, from my bare legs to the curve of my hips to my simple, nude lace bra, before landing on my face. "Beautiful. Everywhere."

My skin hums at his praise.

He inches closer, threads his fingers into my hair. "Feel how hard you make me." He takes my hand from his chest and places it over the bulge in his pants. "You have no idea how long I've wanted you."

"Pshh. The tiniest fraction of your life," I breathe. "You *are* ten years older."

"Means I know how to make you mine."

My hand wraps around his length through his pants. His grin fades, his gaze flaring with heat.

I unfasten his shirt one button at a time,

pushing it off his shoulders. He tosses it to the floor without looking.

What's between us might not end well, but I've never felt the rush I feel around him—outside of the booth.

I'm willing to take this chance...

As long as he'll let me drive.

I sink to my knees and take him out of his dress pants. He's huge and hard, and I've never salivated for a dick before, but apparently there's a first time for everything.

"I prefer it when—"

"I know how to give a blow job," I retort, earning myself a chastising look.

"I'll enjoy it more if you do it the way I like."

I flip him off, for old times' sake. He grabs my hand and sucks my middle finger into his mouth.

A jolt of pleasure grips my spine as heat wraps around me, settling into a dull ache of pleasure between my thighs.

"Is that a request?" I manage, but his wicked tongue is messing with my head.

"I prefer those hands engaged in more productive pursuits," he rasps when he releases me.

For once, I'm not arguing.

I turn my attention back to his hard cock. I

wrap my fingers around him, using the wetness from his mouth to slide up and down.

His exhale is half-groan and entirely sexy.

I take him in one long ambitious stroke until he hits the back of my throat.

"Fuck, Raegan. Your dirty mouth is so fucking sweet."

He wants to take control. His hand fists in my hair, pushing me down, and I shove him away. Eventually his touch comes back, cupping my face, fingers threading into my hair, thumb brushing my hollowed cheek as I suck him.

Having this kind of power is like the feeling of playing to a huge crowd, only this is better.

"You're preening," he rasps when I pull off him to catch my breath.

"I deserve it."

He drags me to the carpet.

He's filthy rich, but right now, he's just filthy.

His hands stroke down my body as if he's memorizing every inch before his mouth comes back to claim mine. It's brutal, punishing me for every day we've been apart.

His grip finds my throat, and a ribbon of fear snakes through me. But it's overtaken by pleasure as he works a finger inside me. I can't do anything but arch my back and take him deeper.

"So wet."

It's a curse and praise at once.

He drags his cock over my mound, a cruel tease.

I feel as if I've never had him inside me. But before he can make good on his implied promise, he parts my legs and shifts down my body.

"First, you'll beg."

That dirty mouth settles between my legs. If you can call it settling, because he's restless, his tongue and lips moving together to drive me wild with need.

A slow, leisurely lick.

A hard suck.

A rhythm more compelling and brutal than anything I've ever laid down on a track.

My fingers grasp at the carpet, his hair, whatever I can find. "Oh shit."

I could tell him how I usually get myself off, but I can't even think. There's no way to tell him what to change because I wouldn't know how to ask for this if I tried.

He plays my body as though he was born to. Not because the first time he touches me is perfect, but because he takes every shiver of my body, every hitch of my breath, every incoherent murmur from my lips, and uses it against me.

The man is a fucking doomsday machine set out to destroy me, to teach my body to ruin itself.

"Tell me you missed me." His lips vibrate against my skin.

"Your smug elitist mouth? Not likely."

His fingers twist inside me and I gasp, yanking on his hair. He holds me in place.

"My smug elitist mouth is going to make you scream."

When I come, it's a record-setting explosion, even for LA. The aftershocks rack me for seconds, minutes, hard enough my toes ache.

He appears over me, hair mussed, and suddenly he looks ten years younger by virtue of the cocky expression.

I manage to prop myself up on my elbows. "That all you've got?"

His low chuckle is sexy as hell. "On the contrary. Just getting started."

He grabs something from his pants pocket, then graces me with those intense blue eyes while he rolls on the condom.

How I ever thought those eyes were cold I don't know. They're white-hot.

He positions himself at my slit, the head of him bumping where I'm wet and making me ache. He sinks into me, an impossibly thick inch at a time.

So full.

I'm full of him, everywhere. My body, my head, my senses. There's no denying it.

Every instinct to struggle against the invasion ends with my fingers clenching, my body clenching, as he slides deeper.

When his cock hits resistance, I gasp in relief.

The last time we did this, we were swept up by the emotion of the night and needing escape and comfort.

This is intentional.

I told him we had no contract now, but it's not true. We signed on an implicit line tonight, possibly from the moment he sat down at that table.

A promise we'd play this out tonight with clear eyes and clear heads. And this time, neither of us is running.

His groan ends on a hiss, and I realize he's struggling with control as much as I am.

"Feel how deep I am," he rasps in my ear.

"Memorize it. Every second I'm not inside you, you'll wish I was."

Those words send blood pounding through my veins.

"I'm going to cover every damn inch of this body before we're through. But first..." The flash of cockiness in his eyes is the hottest thing I've ever seen. "You'll come for me."

I wrap my legs around his hips, squeezing hard enough to make me gasp and his jaw tighten.

"Don't make promises you can't keep," I pant. "I understand endurance is harder at your age—"

"Just for that, you'll count. Every fucking stroke." He shoves me back, his chest brushing mine so there's no question I'm staying down.

I'd laugh if I wasn't so caught up. I count the first stroke in my head, almost losing track at the firm thrust of him stretching me, the sight of him, a powerful and determined flex of muscle and man over me.

The next second, my butt is on fire, and I yelp. "The fuck?"

His eyes flash with satisfaction. "Count. Out loud."

"Two," I pant, my voice wavering at the edges. The angle is different this time, hitting me where

I'm aching, and the knowing look on his face says he knows.

Still, there's no way I'll...

"Fuck... three..."

My back arches up off the carpet, unbidden.

Harrison's lazy mouth is in direct contrast with the rest of him, descending to leave a trail of heat up my throat.

Unreal.

"Five..."

More, overtaking me.

I'm at twelve when he presses on my clit and I clench around him.

"That's cheating," I mumble as the orgasm crashes through me.

He moves through my climax, harder and faster and relentless. Until his body stills inside me and his muscles seize.

The heavy exhale is torn from deep inside him, his shoulders flexing and eyes squeezing shut.

It's a thing of beauty, watching this tightly laced man fall apart. I can't help tightening around him as he spills himself inside me.

When Harrison collapses over me, he's still in me.

"No fucking clue why people would want to

come at the same time." His dry accent is so close to my ear he might be in my head. "I prefer to watch you."

When his head lifts, he's grinning. My heart skips. He's breathtaking like this. Happy and gorgeous and relaxed, and it reminds me of the strange closeness I felt while we were in Ibiza.

An alarm goes off, and I lift my head in confusion.

My phone.

"I have a show," I state.

"You have a show," he agrees.

When he says it, the meaning sinks in. "Fuck, Harrison, I have a show."

I shift out from under him, shoving both hands through my hair. I start to stand, but there's a hand in my face.

He's already up, helping me.

My phone buzzes, and I find it lying on the floor next to my clothes.

Beck: Heads up that I have a girl staying over tonight. In case you two run into each other naked in the kitchen.

. . .

I'm barely done reading when I notice Harrison reading over my shoulder.

"You never slept with him."

"Is privacy dead?" I complain, lowering the phone to my side.

But he stares me down.

"Beck's really into this girl," I admit as I grab my dress and tug it on.

"Stay over. Come back after your show."

That feels like too much of him—a dangerous amount.

"No."

"You're punishing me for leaving you that night."

Surprise has me jerking toward him. He's only wearing black boxer briefs, his gorgeous body moving easily as he slips on his shirt and fastens the handful of buttons from the bottom.

"You were with me long enough to make me come," I say.

Where is my damn underwear?

Harrison holds up my panties, and I cross to grab them out of his hand.

He holds on. "Just not long enough to make you stay."

I pull harder, and this time, he lets go.

8

HARRISON

*T*exts are meant to be responded to promptly.

They're not an email or a goddamned letter.

But when I text Raegan the next day at noon to say, "I trust you slept well..."

There's no answer.

I wanted her to come back after her set last night. We would've made it two steps in the door before I pressed her up against the wall and her hands were under my shirt. We would have fucked in the living room—again—before she crashed.

But I got out of bed alone this morning, except for memories that made my cock twitch against my leg. I headed for the shower, jerked off for momentary relief.

I'm not finished with her, not by a long shot.

I've never wanted a woman who challenged me on every level. Normally I date beautiful women interested in enjoying life and being enjoyed. Raegan's anything but that.

In the kitchen, I take a moment to miss my housekeeper's cooking before reaching for the fridge door handle. Since I arrived, I haven't opened it once. The hotel chef brings my food himself, and I eat most of it around work—in my office here or at the warehouse with Leni.

Now, I scan the fully stocked shelves.

Juice. Milk. Fresh vegetables, precut. Even chicken.

The pantry contains everything from nut butter to protein powder.

Who knew?

I settle on coffee with the French press I had delivered since I was last here.

If only my problems could vanish as easily as the woman whose scent still lingers in my condo.

The new club, for one.

Leni and the team are full-on into a major renovation, and I need to get the zoning approval so we can open on schedule. The more research I do, the more convinced I am that this is the right time for this operation. It could add significantly to Echo Entertainment's bottom line and its reputation.

I take my coffee and phone out to the wrap-around patio overlooking LA and the ocean beyond, hitting voicemail.

"Boss, it's Leni. I've managed to broker deals for most of the materials we need on short order. But some of the sound equipment is backordered and might push the club opening. Unless we can figure out another solution—"

I hit End, cursing.

And this isn't the only venue in my empire.

I've heard almost nothing from Mischa since he invaded Debajo and I slammed a fist into his face. With anyone else, that would be comforting. With him, it's concerning because it means he's working under the radar.

I have to win La Mer, and the stakes have never been higher. If I don't succeed, I will have disappointed my parents, failed before the man responsible for their downfall.

Which is why I take the offensive position when I dial a contact.

"Christian."

"Good morning, Harrison. I understand you've left us."

"For America, not for the dead," I say dryly. The old man does like his drama. "Acquiring La Mer is still my number one priority. To that end, I've committed to a robust investigation to alleviate any concerns about the legitimacy of my parents' activities."

"You're in Los Angeles. It doesn't seem like a priority."

"On the contrary. I'm sparing no expense." I shift, scanning the horizon. I haven't heard anything conclusive from my investigator yet, but he emailed me a status update with some of the areas he's chasing down. "What I don't know is why it's so important to you."

Christian sighs. "There was a deal that went wrong. A property I was going into along with Mischa Ivanov's company—only your father pulled out. The reason was obvious—it would've interfered with the drug trade. But it lost me millions, cost me an entire month with my family. I missed my eldest daughter's graduation picking up the pieces, and that left a bad taste in my mouth. I need to know who made the call, your father or Mischa's."

"And you think learning whether my father was aware of the drug activity will give you that answer."

"Yes."

I frown, pacing the patio. "You've granted me two months. I will get to the bottom of this."

"The terms are changing. Mischa raised his offer yesterday by a million."

The blood in my veins heats. "My offer was more than fair, and it's untainted. Do you want Ivanov's way of doing business as a stain on your soul? A father, a grandfather, has no reason to carry that burden."

"You have thirty days. Provide me the assurances we discussed and the club is yours."

"What does Ivanov think of this?" I challenge. "He doesn't know, does he?"

Christian clicks off without answering.

9

RAE

*W*hen your requests don't get a response, it's a good idea to escalate.

Sure, doing that with Echo Entertainment and Harrison King landed me an unplanned gig with an unwanted billionaire that sent my world spinning, but that was an anomaly.

Once I saw a social post announcing two new headliners at Wild Fest when I got out of bed at noon after last night's show, I knew I was running out of time.

Despite my verbal jousting matches with Harrison to date, I'm not good with confrontation. But I tracked down one of the Wild Fest organizers and am following her down Santa Monica.

I catch up to Victoria Ames at a stoplight where she's riffling through her handbag, cursing. She knocks it to the ground, and I bend to help pick up the contents.

"Thanks. I have a meeting in an hour, and this wasn't on my schedule."

"Victoria? Don't freak out," I go on when she stiffens. "I'm Little Queen. I was talking with the cofounders about playing Wild Fest but haven't heard from them in awhile."

She relaxes a degree. "I know who you are."

I hold out a lipstick, the two pieces of which have come apart. She frowns.

"Five-second rule?" I suggest.

Her mouth twitches, but she takes the tube from me and recaps it. "Everyone wants to play this festival. We have the best acts in the world lined up. Why are you the right fit?"

"Come to a gig I'm playing in town next weekend and I'll show you."

"Post the details on your social and I'll take a look," she counters.

"I'll send them to you." I pull up the graphic and DM it to her account that I found earlier. I call after her, "You notice anything about the head-liners you've announced so far?"

She slows her steps but keeps walking. "They're all top-100 DJs?"

"They all have dicks!"

I shout it loud enough the entire block looks over.

"A donut break was a good idea," Callie says as we head out the door of the place a few blocks from the charity, our small paper bags in hand, later that afternoon.

"I was in the neighborhood."

"This is LA. No one's ever in the neighborhood."

"I had a meeting about this huge festival, Wild Fest, at Santa Monica and Sepulveda."

"What's there?"

"Nothing, I mean actually on the street corner. I chased down one of the organizers and made her talk to me."

She laughs. "And how did it go?"

"I think she's going to come to my gig in Long Beach next weekend. Which reminds me, I need to confirm specs with them." I frown and make a mental note because I haven't heard from them since returning from Ibiza.

"Well, if Wild Fest doesn't want you, they're nuts. Do you remember when we were in high school? The first gig you played?"

"You held my hand."

"Literally." Callie's lips twitch. "You were shaking."

I'd been mixing my own music for a year when I got the chance to play a party. A friend of a friend —at least a friend of one of the girls who had been my friend at the time.

It had been dark, and I was alone in the back.

Until I took over the booth.

There I could be anyone. I didn't need to justify myself or defend my feelings. All I had to do was play.

"I'm surprised you chased that woman down. You must be desperate. Lurking is more your style than full-on attack."

"Maybe my style is changing." *I'm changing*, I realize as I cut her a look. "I'm opening a club for Harrison King."

My cousin's smile falls away. "What?"

"It's in Burbank. He's not a bad guy, Callie."

"He's a billionaire who lives in the tabloids. Yes, LA is full of people like that. But not ones we hang out with. At least, not who we hung out with growing up," she amends.

"Harrison's intense. He pushes, and with anyone else, I'd tell them to fuck right off. The reason it works is I don't have to live in the past with him."

"Because he doesn't know your past?" she counters.

"Because I don't have to get into that shit. We can have fun."

"Fun?" She arches a brow as I grab her arm.

"Yes. He's fun."

She rolls her eyes, and I laugh.

"You mean the sex is fun."

I pull my donut from the bag, swipe a finger through the icing, and lick it off. "The sex doesn't suck."

Last night at his place was beyond hot. The first time we were together in Ibiza, the sex was desperate and hurried. This time, I got a taste for how he'd be in bed if we were together.

Not that we made it to the bed.

He demanded I fall in line the way he does when we're clothed. The difference is when we're naked, I'm tempted to give that power up to him.

Probably because I know I'll benefit from it in the form of orgasms I could never give myself.

I've never wanted to trust a man with my body or my heart.

That's why when he texted me a few hours ago, I didn't rush to reply. It's not about pretending I'm unavailable. It's about reminding *myself* I'm not available, in the sense that I'm not going to start jumping every time my phone goes off thinking it's him like a teenager with a crush. I want more, but there's a big difference between wanting to christen every surface of his penthouse condo and letting him into my deep, dark secrets.

"I guess I'm protective," my cousin goes on. "This guy dates models and buys clubs and owns yachts—"

"He charters yachts."

"—and you're my cousin. We used to watch South Park and make fun of the preppy snobs and talk about how much better life would be when we didn't have to deal with those people."

"We're having fun," I insist, although my heart beats faster. "I'm not marrying him."

Even if he intended to go there again with a woman, it would probably take the rest of her life just to read the prenup.

Callie nods after a moment. "Speaking of weddings...I'm still surprised you didn't open up to Kian back then."

My fingers tighten, and I drop my donut. "Motherfucker."

"Sorry."

I pick it up and toss it in a nearby trash can. "Kian wouldn't have wanted me to tell him what happened. He'd only feel like shit about it."

The past dredges up feelings of weakness, of powerlessness, and the people who never noticed.

"Maybe he should feel like shit about it." I shake my head. "I know I was giving you a hard time about Harrison, because I can't see you with a guy like that. But if you don't let *anyone* in, you forget how. It's a different kind of pain. A slow one, a subtle one."

I squint into the sun. "You know what'll be a slow, subtle pain? Watching Kian deliver a romantic speech at the wedding."

Callie's laugh almost makes me forget her words.

**Harrison: Need your take on some new
equipment.**

His text is imperious, but since I agreed to play
opening night in exchange for an exorbitant fee, it
makes sense I'd do it.

So, it's before noon the next day when I head to
Burbank.

Despite the dozen trucks in the lot, when I
head in the side doors, only a handful of tradespeople are working. There's no sign of Harrison or
Leni—until a roar goes up from the office, the door
half open. I head that way and see nearly twenty
people gathered around a television screen.

"Wrong time of year for an Oscar party," I
comment.

Harrison crosses to me, doing a slow, thorough
sweep of my figure. "It's Ash's first match of the
year. They refused to keep working once I put it
on, and I don't have the heart to kick them out.
You're out of bed before noon. Are you unwell?"

His firm mouth tips up at the corner, and I
shake my head at his mocking expression.

"I'm fine."

It's not entirely true. Since talking with Callie

about the wedding, I've been spinning over the idea of confronting my past there and what she said about letting people in.

A roar goes up again, and I snap my gaze to the screen. "Who scored?"

"No one," Leni comments. "It was close though."

"That's the noise you make when someone *almost* scores?"

Harrison chuckles, and Leni offers a wry smile. Though I'm not a sports fan, I can tell Ash is really fucking good. He moves the ball easily up the field, passing effortlessly.

"Where's this equipment?"

Harrison brushes a thumb down my cheek before I can stop him. "I'll show you tonight over dinner."

I look around the room. "I thought you wanted me to come look at gear on-site."

"The equipment will be custom order, Raegan," he says as if I'm being deliberately slow. "You inferred I meant here."

"You say jump and I say how high?" I return his stare because, dammit, he could've sent me a link rather than waiting for me to drag my ass down here.

Harrison tugs me to the back of the room. "Let me be clear. I enjoy you. Naked and under me, but all the other ways too. I won't apologize for wanting to see you."

"Being seen together in LA is serious, Harrison."

"Then maybe I'm serious."

His smoldering blue eyes pin me in place, but it's his earnest tone that leaves me speechless.

Images of *TMZ* and *ET* articles splash through my mind. People speculating exactly why we're together. The career I'm trying to build being subordinated to an online dialogue about whether it's a hot affair or whether we're in love. Who I am reduced to a ranking on the "Most Unexpected Couples" list.

I turn away, shoving a hand through my hair before stepping out of the office. He follows, pulling the door after him.

"Whatever you think you want," I say, "it isn't that. Maybe it's companionship. Someone to share your bed who also has your back—"

"Just go the fuck out with me, Raegan."

My chest tightens. There's a question I've been needing to ask, but one that exposes me more that I can stand. "Why me?"

If I expect him to hesitate, he doesn't. "Because under the layers of doubt and questions, you're a woman who knows what she wants and how to get it. The day you see it, I want to be there."

Would it be so bad to fall for Harrison King?

Would he even be there to catch me if I did?

A roar goes up from the other side of the door, and Harrison leans in.

"Now someone scored," Leni calls.

I poke my head in too, and my gaze finds Ash on the screen, a huge grin on his face as teammates carry him up the field.

Something nudges my foot, and I glance down to see Harrison's dress shoe leaning against my sandal.

"What's with the heels?" he murmurs.

"I'm breaking them in to wear for my brother's wedding next month."

His gaze sharpens. "I'm partial to weddings. We met at one, if you recall."

"I chewed you out."

"I loved every second of it."

Part of me blooms, a tiny flower in my chest that's never dared look for the light.

"Wear those tonight when I take you for dinner. I want to fuck you in them." He brushes his lips over mine, and heat streaks straight to my core, settling into a low ache between my thighs.

"Dinner doesn't lead to sex," I say when he pulls back.

"I would never make such a basic assumption about two people as complicated as we are, Raegan."

"Good."

His gaze traces my lips, the same path his mouth just did. "But dinner will lead to fighting. And fighting will lead to sex."

10

HARRISON

I've never found a deal as challenging as the woman sitting in the passenger seat of my car.

"Leni sent me specs, but I must be reading them wrong. All the industry standards are sold out?"

"Correct."

"But if you don't get the best, you'll lose talent," she finishes. "DJs won't want to play."

"It'll take another three months to get the standard installed. The cost in lost revenues is too high. Do you know how much a club like that will make every night it's open?"

"It'll hold two thousand people. Cover, drinks..." She runs through multiple facets of my business and drops a number at the end that's startlingly accurate.

I nearly groan.

Listening to her talk business is sexy.

Which is fucked up because we're talking about how screwed my club is.

"I need to make this work," I mutter. "I will force my way up the supplier list. Find a pressure point and press on it. Whatever Leni did, I'll double down."

"Come on, you didn't ask me to weigh in because you wanted an audience to how you'll go all 'tough guy.' We need to get creative."

I glance at her as we stop at a light. "This isn't MacGyver. I can't use a roll of duct tape and some toilet paper rolls to make a sound system for a high-end venue."

"But venues used other setups before this one was available," she argues. "Hell, you have others in your clubs."

She runs through them while I listen.

Rae is making it difficult to focus. Tonight, she's dressed in the heels from earlier, plus ripped jeans that hug every curve of her legs and hips, a black T-shirt, and oversized sunglasses. She could be a student going to class at UCLA, her hair pulled back in a high ponytail that tickles the headrest of the car when she turns to look at me.

I stare out the windshield as I navigate traffic, but all I'm picturing is twisting that hair around my hand while she comes on my cock.

"What about Blaze?"

I blink. "What's Blaze?"

"The club in Venice Beach. It closed not too long ago, and I heard it's getting sold off and converted into stores."

"You think there's a chance of getting their audio equipment."

"Has to go somewhere." She shrugs. "I could ask."

"Thank you." I read far too much into the fact that she's offering.

She's smart and beautiful. My own damn kryptonite.

It'll be easier when we get to the exclusive beachfront restaurant. A white linen tablecloth between us will keep me civilized.

When we arrive, there's no sign of the valet. I curse, and we park half a dozen blocks away.

"It's fine," Rae says. "Let's walk on the beach."

Most women I've dated would have pouted at having to walk, but she sounds as if she prefers it.

"Coming around to the idea of being seen with me?" I murmur as I hold her door.

"There are worse things."

"When was the last time a man you fucked, or wanted to, took you out for dinner?"

Rae considers as she starts down the sidewalk next to me. I get the feeling she's weighing something bigger than an offhand comment.

"Never."

It's my turn to be stunned.

"That would require someone to ask me," she goes on, "and for me to say yes."

"Endless complexity," I say dryly, but I'm fascinated. "Let's start simple. You tell me what's bothering you. I fix it, or use noncommittal male vocalizations to empathize."

She laughs, and the sound pleases me long after her smile fades once more. "I approached Wild Fest about a spot next spring. One of the recruiters is coming to my show next weekend in Long Beach. It would be a huge deal. They've never had a DJ headline who wasn't in the top twenty of Billboard's Top 100 DJ list."

We start down the concrete steps to the beach.

"I've met the cofounders. I could—"

"Don't you dare intervene for me," she says. "I need to do this on my own."

"Even if it was partly my fault your career was hindered? For the record, I don't feel an ounce of guilt," I go on. "The media will watch you and judge you as if it's their job. Your job is to live your life."

I take the last three steps to the beach as Raegan pauses to pull off her heels. When she straightens, I take advantage of her busy hands to lift her by the waist and set her on the sand in front of me. She's close enough her body brushes mine through our clothes.

"Just because you can do something yourself doesn't mean you should." I skim my hand around to her ass and squeeze lightly. She sways closer, and I bend my lips to her ear. "Goes for all manner of things, love."

When I step back, her eyes are nearly black.

We're surrounded by people, but I wish we were alone.

I want to run my fingers down between her legs, see if she's wet.

"I'll keep that in mind," she murmurs.

With every taste of her, I only want more.

It's startling and unnerving.

Rae's attention drifts past me, and I turn to see a food stand, half a dozen patrons clad in swimming trunks and casual wear waiting to order. I want to recoil on instinct, but she doesn't look away.

Fuck me.

"You want tacos." The three words land heavy in my gut.

"No." Rae turns back, pasting on a quick, false smile I never want to see again. "The restaurant is fine."

I've never been with a woman who didn't want the most elegant things I could give her. Rae's differences are challenging to understand, but I want to try.

That's why I pull out my phone.

"What are you doing?" she demands.

"Texting the concierge to cancel." When I'm done, I hold out a hand for her shoes. "If we're going to eat at a restaurant with a queue, at least I can carry these for you like a gentleman."

"You don't have to."

"Too damn bad."

She hands them over, but the wry shake of her head has me frowning as we take our spot at the end of the queue.

What is she saying—no one's ever been a gentleman with her?

Fuck.

"No more shop talk tonight," I decide, and she arches a brow.

"That a rule?"

"Yes. Besides, you might have already solved the equipment problem."

She grins, and I can't help but return it.

I want to show her something different.

We order tacos and find a spot to sit on the beach. Before Rae can sit, I spot a beach hut where I can purchase a towel embroidered with crabs so we can eat without getting sand in our food. Ash would piss himself laughing if he could see me now. We talk about all kinds of things.

"Most embarrassing moment?" I ask.

"A show in New York during arts school. I was mixing from my notebook, and it tried to run an update installation midcycle."

I laugh silently.

"What about you? I have a hard time picturing you embarrassed."

"Fuck, there are loads," I insist, scanning my memories. "Oh. Initiation the first year of boarding school, we were at the beach, and some other boys stole my swimsuit. I had to walk back to the dorms with a piece of food wrap"—I hold up the paper from my taco—"to cover myself and explain to the headmaster why I was out without a uniform."

Her shoulders rock with laughter. The humiliation was worth it for this one moment.

"Favorite TV show?" she asks once she's recovered.

"*Great British Bake Off.*"

"You're lying."

"Am not," I insist. "And if you so much as think of telling another human, you won't live long enough to do it. What's yours?"

"*South Park.*"

I shake my head. "Unbelievable."

"That I like a cartoon?"

"Mhmm."

No. That I'm falling for a woman who likes a cartoon. I finish my taco, mostly managing to avoid dropping coleslaw on the sand.

"Proudest moment?" she asks me.

I don't have to think about it. "I've bought my share of venues, but I was twenty-five when I opened the first one I built from scratch. The moment we turned on the sign and those lights lit up the night, I swear I could feel my parents watching me. It was the first time I felt as if I was doing the right thing."

Rae studies me without blinking. "Well, that's intense. What was it called?"

"Brillante."

"I'm surprised you didn't name it something more personal."

"It never occurred to me," I say honestly. "Would you have? You never stay in one place long enough for anything to become personal."

"If it was a building, brick and mortar... I think I would."

I turn that over before asking my next question. "Most awkward sexual encounter?"

Rae knocks over her drink with a knee, cursing as she rights it. "I don't want to talk about it."

So, I change the subject, but I'm still wondering why that simple question threw off our conversation.

"I've never been to the beach in LA," I admit as I reach for the mineral water I bought.

"Seriously? How many times have you come here?"

"Dozens."

"Huh. I'm glad I can give you a first."

I reach a hand out to lift her chin. Then I lean in and brush my lips across hers.

She tastes like her soda, and I want to drink her dry. I want to lay her back on this towel and strip off her clothes and show her how fucking exquisite she is.

Instead, I allow her to finish her dinner before I walk her back to the car.

"Aren't we going back to your place?" she asks when I drive us away from my side of the city.

"No."

She looks over in surprise. "Why not?"

I'm torn between a laugh and a groan. "You've never had a gentleman. I wanted to give you a first too."

Her eyes soften in the twilight, and I grab onto that as my hands clench the steering wheel. She flicks on the radio, humming to the music as we drive.

I've never had someone I can coexist with. But her, right here... it feels surprisingly right.

Except for the blood diverted below my belt at the sound of her voice or any time I glance at her.

When I pull up to Beck's gates and put the car in park, she turns to face me.

"You can come in. But you can't stay ov—"

"No."

She blinks at me in surprise.

Her palm slides down my chest, rubbing across my erection through my pants. My body leaps under her touch. "You still want to be a gentleman?"

She's teasing me. I like seeing her empowered.

No.

"Yes."

Her hand threads through mine as she tugs me toward her.

I follow her lead, mostly because I have no idea what she's planning.

When she works open the button and fly of her jeans and slides my hand inside, I swallow my tongue.

She's slick and ready for anything I might wish to do to her. Knowing she was getting turned on by our conversation, by simply spending time together, blows my mind.

I rub a slow circle over her clit beneath her underwear, and her eyelids fall to half-mast as she arches against my touch.

"I want to see you tomorrow," I mutter.

Rae squirms, a noise of tortured pleasure escaping her lips before she answers, "No."

The fuck?

My fingers slip inside her heat.

First one, then a second.

My cock chafes against the zipper of my trousers. "The next day."

I could be free of these trousers in a minute. Inside her in two. Making her scream my name loudly enough her smug roommate can hear.

But I want to show her she means more to me than sex. I want her to trust me, to know that I want more of her. I want all of her.

"I'm busy this week," she pants, gripping my wrist as I slowly pump her with my fingers. "Working on this set."

She's letting me in physically but pushing me away emotionally.

I can't use my normal approach of pinning her down. Brute force does nothing with this woman. She turns to vapor.

It takes everything in me to withdraw my hand, leaving behind her sweet, tight heat. "I'm going to add you to my calendar. You look at it and let me know when you're available."

If it takes her more than three damn days, I'll be back over here. But I don't say that.

Raegan blinks in surprise, shoving at a chunk

of hair that's fallen out of her ponytail. "You don't know what you're missing."

"I know exactly what I'm missing." I suck her off my fingers, and her jaw drops. "And what I got tonight is worth even more."

My balls ache the entire way home.

11

RAE

"*I* Can't Feel My Face" streams out of my headphones, but it's my feet that've gone numb. Ernie's been lying on them for an hour while I sit on Beck's patio and work on my set for Long Beach.

I drum my fingers on the arm of the chaise, reviewing the set list.

When I approached them with the midsummer "zombie beach" theme a couple months ago, they were down with it. Though I'm still waiting on a final equipment confirmation, it's going to be great.

It has to be because Victoria said she'd come, and this is my chance to prove I deserve a spot at Wild Fest.

I gently move Ernie onto the patio despite his whine of protest. The track changes, and I shut my eyes to listen.

The dog licks my bare calves, and I hold out the headphones. "It's really fucking good, right?"

He sniffs them gingerly, his wet nose flaring.

"Don't tell Beck I was swearing around you. He thinks you're too impressionable."

Light glints off the diamonds set into each earpiece, the band connecting them. They're always with me now.

And so, it seems, is the man who gave them to me.

Harrison took me for dinner on the beach two nights ago. We ate tacos and talked about stupid bullshit that somehow felt important because of the man I shared it with. Seeing the billionaire relax enough to sit on the sand and laugh affected me. It made me think about how things could be, if I let them.

He's the one pushing us forward, pushing us closer. He peels back parts of me, even without words.

It's disconcerting.

By the time we were done with our food, I was having a really good time. Plus, I was looking forward to seeing him put his beautiful body to better use. When he drove me back to Beck's and told me good night, I nearly died.

I don't know if the way he fingered me in the car made it better or worse.

After cursing him in the foyer, I finally gave in, went upstairs, and made myself come twice, imagining his dirty mouth on me, his fingers inside me.

No matter what I felt while we were eating tacos and talking about his childhood antics, I'm not handing my heart to a man whose primary directive is to claim and conquer.

I grab a snack and return to the chaise as an email pops up. I read it twice.

Re: Next Weekend's Show

We apologize for the delay in responding to your request. It is no longer in our mutual interest to retain you for the engagement. Of course, we don't expect the deposit to be returned to us.

We look forward to collaborating in the future.

. . .

The club where I was booked to do my Zombeach just bailed on me.

This is not a small problem. It's a huge one.

I check their feed, and they've already swapped out my name for someone else's on the poster. Disbelief rises up. *What the actual fuck?*

I put all that effort into getting Victoria to this show, and I've been working on the set for two days straight.

I could curl up in a corner and squeeze my eyes shut and wait for the waves of emotion to rack me.

I could see Beck at the lot. He'd cheer me up, tell me not to sweat it.

Or I could call Annie in New York, who'd no doubt encourage me to make them see my side of things with some impassioned plea.

I don't want either.

This is Harrison's fault.

He insisted on giving me access to his calendar, which I haven't enabled on my phone. Now, I click into my calendar on my phone and check the box that syncs Harrison's calendar.

Events start to populate, dozens this week alone. There are meetings and calls and dinners and invitations at all hours of the day and night. Some of them even overlap.

I had no idea how busy running his empire really is. But it looks like he has a break in thirty minutes.

All I need is to see him. I want to chew him out. To say this is all his damn fault and my life was better before he entered it.

So, I drive to his penthouse, and the concierge lets me up.

"Harrison?" I call into the condo when I step inside.

There's no answer, and I stalk toward the office. "I'm not here for sex," I warn.

When I round the door, I pull up as I see two other men in suits inside, in addition to the man I'm here to see.

Three startled gazes fly to me, including one that's amused as it is surprised.

Shit.

"I didn't mean..." I hold up my phone. "I thought you had a break between meetings."

"Raegan. Wait." Harrison comes after me, catching up to me before I reach the elevator in the hall. "What's wrong?"

His gray suit is perfectly pressed, his jaw

freshly shaved. He's as composed as I am wrecked, and the contrast has never felt so obvious as it does in this moment.

"The show I was supposed to play in Long Beach next weekend. They canceled it. Someone from Wild Fest was coming and..."

His probing gaze is compassionate. Genuinely caring. "Don't move."

He goes back into the penthouse before retuning with a sheaf of papers he hands to me.

"What are these?" I ask, flipping through the pages.

"A list of clubs with contact information. These are my competition. They're not all as shortsighted as the one you spoke with today."

I didn't come here for him to fix it. I came here to yell at him, but I can't. Now that I'm here, that's not what I want at all.

My chest tightens, and I step closer, folding the list in half and tucking it into my bag. The backs of my eyes burn.

"It's not fair." I sound like a kid but can't bring myself to care.

"No. It's fucking not."

He threads his fingers into my hair at the nape

of my neck—to comfort, not to arouse. When he pulls me to his chest, I don't resist.

His arms go around me, and I can't deny how good it feels to be held by him.

Maybe I didn't come to yell at him. Maybe what I wanted even more was to look him in the eye and have him tell me I matter and all the reasons we shouldn't be together don't matter.

"Come inside," he murmurs against the top of my head. "My meeting ran late. I'll end it now."

"You don't have to. Your calendar is full, and—"

"It's only business." His mouth brushes over mine. Soft, not clinging.

"Never be ashamed to ask for what you want. If I can give it to you, it's yours."

***

"She's not answering," Harrison mutters from where his head's stuck in the cabinet. Phone glued to his ear, he searches out the perfect pan.

"Let me look online. There's got to be a good paella recipe."

"It's not the same. Natalia used to make it for us as boys. Ash loved it as much as I did, even helped make it." Harrison rises from his crouched position, bumping his head on the counter on the way. "Fuck."

I head to the freezer and pull out some ice, wrapping it in a towel.

He accepts it with a grimace. "I'm a dangerous man."

"It's occasionally sexy. Why don't you wear casual clothes?"

"I used to, but my father told me before I went to boarding school as a teenager, 'If they're going to catch you with your pants down, at least ensure your cufflinks are fastened.'"

I turn that over. "Well, no one is going to see you here. At least lose the dress shirt."

He peels it off, leaving an undershirt beneath. "Better?"

Now I'm staring. "You could put something else on."

"No. No, I think you're right. You should take something off too."

"Strip cooking isn't a thing."

"Just because it hasn't made it to America..."

"Oh. It's all over *GBBO*?" I roll my eyes and tug off my jeans. My underwear is a pair of plain black bikinis since I didn't plan on being here, so I'm basically still covered everywhere that counts. "There."

Harrison's gaze tracks unapologetically south, skimming the curves of my legs before lingering at the apex of my thighs.

"Where were we?" he murmurs.

"Tracking down Natalia's paella recipe."

I snap my fingers in front of his face, and his amused gaze flicks up to meet mine.

"Ah. It may be a lost cause. We could move to another of my preferred activities when I've had a terrible day."

"Jerking off?"

"An excellent idea. But not where I was going. Sometimes I take Barney out. He reminds me things are simpler in his world."

"He's in Ibiza?" A nod. "He must miss you."

"Toro and Natalia take good care of him when I travel."

"We could borrow Beck's dog. But let's not give up on comfort food yet." I pull out my phone, then hit a FaceTime contact I haven't used in months.

I'm not seriously expecting an answer, so when Sebastian appears on the screen, the movement of a city street behind him, I'm delighted.

"Hey, Ash," I say.

"Raegan. To what do I owe the pleasure?"

Harrison's brows shoot up. "Why do you have my brother's number?" he mouths. He looks like a jealous teen, and I wave him off.

I say, "This a good time?"

"Sure, I'm heading home from practice."

"We're trying to make Natalia's paella."

He grins. "You with Harry? Or is this an attempt to impress some new boyfriend?"

Harrison grabs the phone from my hand. "I'm here, you prick. Now talk chorizo."

"Thought you'd never ask." His handsome face scrunches up, then he comes out with the ingredients.

I make notes on a piece of paper. We're going to have to go out and get these or have them delivered. There's tension between the two men, which I want to know more about.

"We watched your game the other day," I say.

"Match," they correct in unison.

"Right. It looked good. Does that mean things are going better?"

He freezes as if caught out. "Work in progress. I should let you get back to your activities."

After we hang up, I probe Harrison. "What's with the tension?"

"Since our parents died, he doesn't see me the same way he used to. He knows it's my fault they're not around."

"He got you a dog after you broke up with your fiancée. That means he cares."

"Or he wanted to punish me. He doesn't think I have a soul," Harrison says darkly. "He figured a dog would out me."

"And you proved him wrong."

His slow smile has my heart skipping.

"You don't talk about your family," he comments.

"A lot of people I trusted let me down when I needed them."

He brushes a hand through my hair. "Tell me what happened."

"Hard pass. You're not my therapist."

I try to make it sound light, but he doesn't smile.

"Listen," I go on, turning to pace the room, "despite the whole 'crashing your workday' thing, I'm not spending time with you because I need a well-tailored shoulder to cry on."

When I turn back to him, he's already closed the distance between us.

"There are moments in our lives that defy

description. Sometimes we cause them and sometimes we don't. But they are painful and incomprehensible, and pretending they're not doesn't make us more human. I need people around me. Leni, and Toro, and Natalia, and even Ash. You need to let someone in."

The openness in his voice and his face is undeniable. He's lived through his share of shit, but even if I wanted to invite him into mine, he can't possibly understand.

"Well, this army of one thing has been working out for me so far." I force my attention to the shopping list. "Should we go out and get these?"

It's an obvious subject change, and I think he's going to argue.

"Let's have them delivered."

He places the order with the concierge, who promises to have all we need delivered in an hour. When Harrison tugs me toward the doors to the deck, I follow.

On a chaise, he tucks me between his legs. "What are you going to do about Wild Fest?"

"Well, I have to tell Victoria the gig's off. But I saw on their page they have a dark horse spot. Basically, fan votes," I go on at his questioning look.

"Are you in the running?"

I pull it up on my phone and make a face. "Twenty-fifth. There's one spot." I frown. "I'm playing in Miami on Thursday. If I can get enough fans to share the show, it'll be a boost."

"I'm visiting my club there Friday, plus I could use the change of scenery. Give Leni a few days to work on this warehouse without me. Suppose I could head over early."

"You'd come to my show? At someone else's club?" I ask, surprised. Every part of me hums with anticipation. The idea of him watching me is thrilling.

"You going to ask me?"

My lips twitch, and I fight the impulse to smile, squaring my shoulders. "Come to my show, asshole."

"Fuck, you're irresistible."

But when he drags me against him, I can't help laughing.

12

RAE

*H*avana Nights looms on Collins Avenue in Miami, an art deco monument. I'm at the bar early to set up.

I need this gig in order to make my case for Wild Fest. Most of all, I need the line of partiers to vote for me. Normally, I wouldn't ask for that kind of help, but I'm desperate. So, I hired someone to make graphics encouraging my fans to vote.

The club is full, Harrison talking to the owner and some patrons in one of the VIP booths. Of course he made himself at home.

The crowd is mostly people who want to escape for the night. I give them every ounce of my focus, sweat and attention.

I catch Harrison's eye once, and I'm rewarded

with a long, smoldering look of appreciation that adds to the high of being onstage.

When he finally turns away to speak with someone, I notice another man in the adjacent VIP booth watching me over the rim of his drink. Unlike his buddies, he hasn't averted his eyes once in the last two songs.

I play my mind out. At the end of my set, I sneak a look at the voting for Wild Fest on my phone as I duck offstage.

Twenty-third. It's a minor blip. But people can vote more than once. Ten times in a twenty-four-hour period, technically. Which means every person in line for selfies is that much more important.

"Two minutes," I shout to security before ducking out back.

I need to catch my breath before heading back in.

The alley is a reprieve—no cooler than inside, but I inhale deeply anyway.

I'm going over what went down in my mind, reliving it with a breathless smile in this moment of privacy until movement at the mouth of the alley draws my attention.

A large, dark form.

Harrison.

I start to call out, but as he comes closer, I realize it's not Harrison.

This man's coarse where Harrison is sleek, jerky where he's smooth.

"I was watching you in there. Making everyone want you."

He wedges up against me, and I can't breathe. My heart explodes.

"I thought you were someone else," I manage.

"Come on. You want this."

Really fucking don't.

There's a chance to lunge under his arm and run for the street, but I'm a second late and his hand goes around my throat and cuts off my air.

I grab for his wrist, fingernails digging into his skin. He flinches but doesn't let go.

An icy sheet of fear slices me in two.

It's not like what happened with Mischa. I was freaked but knew someone was only a breath away.

This is dark. No one is here.

The sounds of the party are distant, and no matter how strong I am on the inside, all that matters is this man's grip.

"Miss?" security calls into the alley from way too far away.

I can't speak, can't breathe. I wave my hands, trying to signal.

"Hey!"

The man pulls back, and I shove at him and duck away, staggering down the alley toward the club entrance.

My surroundings are a blur. I trip inside, looking both ways, and find my way back to the green room.

I press my head between my knees and gulp air.

I need space.

"Raegan. Are you all right?"

Harrison's voice comes from above me, but I don't look up.

"What the hell happened?" he barks but not at me.

"A man approached her outside. Seems it triggered... this."

Security radios the manager, whose voice I hear a moment later.

"I'll take it from here," Harrison says.

I'm swept into the back of a car, the leather

seats worn yet too formal for the rawness eating me from the inside out.

I want to scream.

I want to die.

I wrap my arms around my knees and do neither.

Harrison

She's gone.

Raegan is gone, and the woman curled in the back of the limo is someone I don't know. Her cheeks shine with tears, her dark lashes blinking rapidly as she stares at the floor.

"Did he hurt you?" I ask, trying to keep my voice low and calm for her benefit. Inside, I'm enraged and worried.

She shakes her head once.

He might not have hurt her, but he scared the hell out of her.

Management said they'd captured the man

and that he didn't have a weapon. Which means he terrified her with his body or his words.

She's swaying with the motion of the car, and I lean forward to tell the driver to keep driving. It seems to be helping, or at least not hurting.

"Raegan," I say when I return to her, kneeling on the floor so I'm beneath her. "This happened before."

She doesn't answer.

"At my club?" I barely force out the words.

A slow headshake.

But my negligence did this—worse than this—to other women. Regret is heavy in my gut, a roiling grief that won't relent.

"A long time ago," she says at last.

She's so fucking young now. That someone met her years before, wanted her, hurt her—it makes me murderous.

"I don't talk about it." Her grip on her knees tightens.

My fingers dig into the seat upholstery to keep from ripping the roof off the car. "If you tell me now, I won't ask you to again."

I need to know what happened. I can't stand her keeping secrets, not only because I'm used to having full information, but because they're eating her alive.

Her glassy eyes scan the street beyond the window. "I don't want you to look at me differently."

What the fuck?

"There's nothing you could say that would change how I look at you."

Her gaze finds mine, and it's full of fear. "Are you sure?"

"Yes."

She takes a slow breath. "It was sophomore year, and my brother was having a party with some friends from campus. My parents were gone for the weekend. There was a guy from his class— older, preppy, good looking. Like my brother, he'd gone to our high school, and a lot of the girls had a thing for him. I thought I did too. Until I didn't.

"We were under the deck outside, drinking. He kept saying I wanted it, and I kept telling myself maybe I did, but it wasn't true."

The streetlights fly past the window, but I don't bother to look out. I'm numb to everything but the woman in front of me.

"Did he rape you?"

The voice sounds like mine, but I don't remember forming the question.

"Yes."

I die.

A piece of my soul shrivels up, but my heart keeps beating because she keeps talking, and I need to be here for her. With her.

"There are parts of the night I remember, and others I don't. I woke up in my bed. I was..." She swallows. "I was sore."

Fuck. "He slipped something in your drink."

A nod. "I went over it a hundred times. That's the only thing I can come up with. I remember not wanting to be part of it. But the party was thirty feet away, and I didn't scream. I didn't do anything."

"Did you report him?" My voice is even, as if listening to what she's saying doesn't make me feel as if I'm being burned alive.

None of it matters. I'm focused on her.

"I went to the police station but couldn't go through with it. I didn't tell my parents, not at first. But the burden got to be too much to keep it inside. I struggled in school. Couldn't sleep. Stopped eating. When I admitted to my parents what happened, they fought over what to do about it. My mother wanted to have him charged and expelled from school. My father disagreed."

If my teeth clench any harder, they might break. "How is that possible?"

"It's not the way it sounds. The guy was from a connected family. My dad didn't like seeing me hurt, and he thought reporting it would hurt me more. He tried to fix it in his own way. Got me a new computer. A synth. I wasn't able to do anything productive, so I threw myself into making music.

"It was something I could do when I couldn't do anything else. I'd spend hours working on tracks. Mixing and mastering. I didn't need to act a certain way. I didn't need to feel a certain way. I could put my headphones on and drown out the world. Hell, sometimes I could even drown out my thoughts."

My chest is raw, scraped down to my ribs.

I wanted to know her.

I didn't expect *this*.

"When I stopped going out to parties, my supposed friends decided I wasn't interesting anymore. The one person who believed me and didn't leave me or make me feel like an outcast was my cousin, Callie."

I hate that Rae suffered that kind of torture, and I hate that she kept this to herself. No wonder she doesn't trust anyone to take care of her.

"I have one more question." My voice is surprisingly even considering I'm a second from burning down the world. "Who was he?"

Before she can answer, her phone buzzes. She glances at the notifications.

"Fans are pissed I didn't stay for selfies." She curses. "I needed those extra Wild Fest votes. Did you know you can vote ten times in a twenty-four-hour period?"

It's totally irrelevant given what went down. But it's not irrelevant to her. She's focusing on something she feels she can control to block out the grief. I know what that feels like. I did it after my parents died, channeling every part of me into building an empire.

I grab my phone and navigate to the Wild Fest page. "Here?"

She presses her lips together, nodding. "But you have to create an... account."

Her voice trails off as I complete the signup. Then I vote for Little Queen, one time after another.

When I'm done, I tuck the phone away and

look up to find her watching me. In her dark eyes and pressed-together lips, I see a semblance of Raegan returning.

"I'd like to stay with you tonight," I say. "I'll sleep on the couch. The floor. Whatever makes you feel safest."

"I don't need that." Rae exhales heavily, and her feet descend toward the floor on either side of me.

My chest contracts as I take her in, a long sweep. "I do."

Rae

When we get out at the mid-rise boutique hotel, Harrison lets me go first. Not because he's being a gentleman. Because he's concerned. It's written on every inch of his handsome face, every tense line of his body.

I told him a secret I never meant so share. One I buried so far down it hasn't seen the light of day in years.

And we can't go back.

Tonight was my chance to make a statement that I'm worthy of Wild Fest. But by this time tomorrow, there'll be a ton of comments about how I left without saying goodbye and no more votes.

Nothing was gained, and it feels like something huge was lost.

The elevator gets to my floor and the doors slide open, but he doesn't move.

I brush past him. "You should go." He planned to stay in Miami for longer, so he booked a penthouse on the ocean a few miles north of the one my gig secured for me. "I'm going to take a bath and go to bed."

"I'm not leaving."

My hands clench into fists. "I mean it. Fucking leave."

"You were right," he says from behind me, and I pause near my door. "Tonight changed something between us."

My eyes squeeze shut. This is what I was afraid of. Our relationship has been filling a void I'd told myself didn't need filling.

And now it's over.

I reach for the key and slip it into the lock.

"I understand why you don't let people in. I can't promise to make up for all of them, Raegan. But I'll fucking die trying."

The raw confession as he steps toward me has my heart thudding against my ribs.

I let go of the key and turn slowly, the carpet soundless under my feet.

He fills the hallway in his dark suit. Somewhere along the way, he lost the tie. The blue of his eyes is like a stormy sea. His throat works, his scent washing over me as he closes the distance between us.

I trust him more than I ever thought I would. But he's asking for more. To be let in when I'm vulnerable, when all I want to do is shut out the world.

I reach for the key once more, pushing in the door before pausing.

"You can sleep on the couch."

13

HARRISON

I can't remember the last time I slept on a sofa.

But I am now, springs digging into my sides and my feet hanging off the end. I've never humbled myself like this for a woman. If tonight's events weren't enough to keep me awake, the discomfort would be. Somehow, though, I manage to fall asleep, because the next time I blink my eyes open, there's movement by the door to the bedroom.

I shift onto my elbow, ignoring the pain in my neck from sleeping on a throw pillow. "Raegan?"

She approaches without a word and stops next to the sofa. Her hair is braided over one shoulder after her bath, an oversized T-shirt covering her body.

"How much is sleeping on that couch killing you?" she murmurs.

"Never better," I lie.

In the dark, I can't see her face, but she holds out a hand. I lace my fingers through hers, running my thumb across her skin.

"C'mon." Rae tugs me to standing.

I'm awake in an instant, following her toward the bedroom. I fell asleep in shorts, my suit draped across a chair. The hairs on my chest lift in the cool air as we cross to the bed.

My eyes adjusting to the dark, I stare at the dent on the right side of the king bed and chuckle.

"We sleep on the same side, don't we?" she asks.

"It would be too easy if we didn't." I stroke her hand with my thumb. "I'll wrestle you for it."

This time it's definitely a laugh.

She turns toward me, our hands still linked.

"Tell me how to help you," I murmur.

She's quiet a moment, as if no one's ever asked her that. "After a show, I can lie awake for hours. Sometimes, in my head, I wind up back at that party as a teenager. No matter how many years or gigs or miles I put between myself and that night, I can't forget it. I don't want to be there. I want to be here, with you."

I've always needed purpose, and the trust on her face gives me a new one.

I inch closer until she's a breath away. She doesn't move.

My lips caress hers. Gentle, simple, without the intent to tease or arouse. She sighs against me, her palm flattening against my bare abs, making me tighten under her touch.

I kiss her like I've never kissed a woman, but then everything is a challenge with her. Even taking things slow with her is torture. Her tongue brushes mine, and my cock hardens.

I meant what I said. Something did change tonight.

Just not what she thought.

I back her toward the bed until her knees hit the sheets.

She breaks our kiss. "You still want me."

There's no inflection at the end, but it's a question. Every inch of her body, the trembling of her lips, tells me it is.

"I wake up wanting you." I drag the shirt over her head. "I go to sleep wanting you."

Her soft curves have me aching, and I slide my hands to touch her breasts with nothing between us.

"I breathe, I fucking want you."

Her eyes are wide, cheeks flushed, and lips already bruised from mine. "Show me."

I don't know how to fix her, but there's nothing to be fixed. She's made the way she is. Like me, she's a combination of everything that's happened to her.

She's not broken. She's beautiful.

A piece of art as exquisite for its flaws as its perfections.

"I'm not going to let you out of this bed."

"All night?" she asks.

"Ever."

I spread her knees so I can stand between them, her eyes darkening. I want to leave every part of her swollen and humming. Use every part of myself to worship her and every trick I've ever learned.

My body is tight everywhere, already anticipating my release, but it's a long time away. I'll make her lose her mind first, to see only me when she closes those beautiful eyes.

Her nipples are hard in the cool air, and I bend

to suck one. Rae's head falls back, her hair splayed out like dark silk on the duvet.

"Every time I make you come, you say my name."

She snorts. "Seems redundant. Unless you're worried I'm picturing Daniel Kaluuya when I close my eyes. He is handsome and British…"

I bite her and am rewarded by a yelp and her hand tightening in my hair. I want her to trust me to make her feel things. To not run away from me.

I start with her breasts, licking and sucking until she's breathing roughly. Then I skim down her body, kneeling between her legs to press my mouth to where she's hot and wet.

The lace is rough, and her flesh is slick and smooth. I would tear it off except that it's frustrating her every bit as much as me, and that's my goal.

I grab the side of her thong and draw it up, pulling so it tightens everywhere, leaving lines in her skin and making her slit puff against the lace.

My other hand slides up to rub her breast, tracing a thumb around her nipple before pinching. I suck on her until she breaks, shaking and shivering.

"Say it." I trace a finger up the inside of her thigh, and she trembles from the climax.

"I'm not even naked—"

I press my tongue against her once more where she's sensitive, and she squirms, but I don't let her inch away.

"Harrison. Okay?"

I shift over her, the dazed expression on her face and the fact that her eyes are glazed with pleasure instead of haunted telling me I'm on the right track. She traces her nails down my chest and stomach. I love it enough that I hate what I need to do next.

"Flip."

With a suspicious look, she does.

The sight of her arse in the air has me biting my tongue. I run both hands over her, squeezing and admiring how good she feels as much as the little sound of pleasure that escapes her.

I brush the hair back from her ear. "I'm going to fuck you now."

"You didn't last long."

"Not with my cock. Need to leave something to look forward to."

The underwear stays on, and the next time she

comes, it's around two of my fingers, my thumb pressing hard against her clit.

"Harrison," she pants against the duvet, her hands fisting in the fabric.

She shifts to look over her shoulder, eyes full of hazy pleasure and accusation as I lick her off my fingers.

"How many more times can you come?"

Her sigh is tortured. "None."

I press my lips to the base of her spine. "So much to learn."

I rip the lingerie off her hips, ignoring her gasps as I plunge two fingers back inside her, adding a third when she's rocking toward me even as her legs shake.

My mouth finishes her off, and she cries out against the sheets, her sounds muffled.

"Can't hear you," I rasp.

"Harrison."

I shift her up the bed and onto her back, lifting her knees and instructing her to hold them there. "Again."

The next time, her toes tighten around my neck as I suck on her, my hands squeezing her ass.

"Stop," Rae pants, one hand fisted in my hair to

hold me away as she scrambles back toward the headboard.

I firmly pry her fingers away, pinning them at her side.

"Why?" I ask.

"It hurts."

"Physically or because you're not used to someone putting you first?"

"Both."

It's devastating she's never had anyone take care of her, even though the woman she's become through that independence is admirable.

I want to be that man.

I bend down to press my lips to hers.

When I pull back, I reach for my trousers to grab a condom, but her cool touch on my arm stops me.

"We don't have to."

"You want to stop?"

Not being inside her after what we've done might kill me. My cock aches, leaking more every time she moans and writhes through a climax I dragged her to.

"No, I mean you don't have to use protection. I'm on the pill. Have you...?"

I don't answer because I'm stunned silent.

My muscles are tight, as if I've been worked over rather than her.

"Yes. I've been tested."

Relief washes over her, and she moves first, her lower lip caught between her teeth as she tugs down my shorts.

I rise and kick them off before shifting back over her, leveraging myself over her body with my elbows. Lowering until we're skin to skin, heat to heat.

I move between her thighs, nudging them wider and grazing her wetness to feel her tremble. The head of my cock slides against her soaked flesh, and the feel of her makes me groan.

Man on his knees.

That's what this would be called.

Because as I grab her hip and sink inside her, one inch at a time, I am fucking *fallen*.

She trusted me tonight, and that tells me we're going to be okay. Everything else, the club, I can handle. The greatest gift I've ever gotten is the one she's given me.

Not sharing her body with me, but her life. Her hopes. Her fears.

I'll guard her with every shred of my being.

I let us both adjust, her to the stretch, me to the exquisite tightness.

I draw back, all the way to the tip, on an inhale. And on my exhale, I sink back in.

The curves of her body are addictive, demanding my attention. But I can't look away from her eyes as my thrusts grow deeper.

"You're a goddess."

I'm on the edge, ready to explode.

"I'm a queen," she corrects with a breathless smile.

We come at the same time.

I've never wanted it, never understood why it would matter for our bodies to agree even when our lips couldn't.

With her, it's everything.

After, she lets me hold her in the dark.

"You're my queen," I murmur as I brush the hair from her face.

But she's already asleep.

"We can't let it go for that amount."

The manager at Blaze turns away from me and Leni, marking something off on his clipboard.

When I told Leni I'd made a call about buying the former club's audio equipment after returning from Miami, she agreed to come for a meeting. I decided to tag along in case I could help and because I needed a few hours away from my own thoughts.

I chase the manager, Leni hot on my heels. "It's a good offer for used gear, Tony. Wouldn't you rather it go to another club?"

"I'm not the owner. But if I were him, he'd say

fuck no. Why should someone else succeed at this game when Blaze got squeezed out?"

It's petty, and I'm still turning that over as Leni sidles up.

"Listen, friend." She flashes teeth, but I'm not sure it's a smile. "This place is being demolished. It's being taken apart around you."

And it is—as we speak, tradespeople are passing through, taking measurements to convert this into whatever it will be.

"In a few months, it'll be like this was never here. Your owner might not give a shit because he's onto the next investment. But you do. If some of your crew need jobs?" She holds out a card. "You can send them my way. Sick days. Flexible shifts. I'll treat them right."

He takes the card from her, considering.

But I'm watching Leni. Dressed in shorts and a floral-printed tank top, she doesn't look like the right-hand man to a billionaire. But the intensity on her face sets her apart.

"If you can add a few thousand to your offer and promise you'll interview my staff," Tony says slowly, "I'll go to work on the owner."

This time, Leni's smile is genuine. "You do that."

As we head out into the sunshine, rounding the back parking lot to Leni's beat-up Jetta, I'm still turning over what happened.

She shifts into the driver's side, and I get in opposite her.

"How did you end up working for Harrison?"

Leni laughs as we pull out of the parking lot and slip into the glut of traffic. "That is a long-ass story."

"Will you tell me?"

My visit to Miami had started on a high before taking a rough turn. That man in the alley reminded me of things I've tried to leave behind.

But Harrison wouldn't let me run from myself or the memories.

He wrapped strong arms around me and refused to budge.

From the moment I woke up in that bed alone, I knew I wanted him with me. I hadn't planned on sex and sure as hell didn't plan on skipping the condom.

The fact that we did was one more wall coming down between us.

What happened physically was beyond anything I've experienced, though I'm not about to tell him.

It's always felt like two steps forward and one step back with us, but lately, it's only forward. I keep waiting for him to pull away, but every vulnerability, every moment, he moves into it. Occupies it as naturally as if he's always been in my life and my heart.

I'm consumed by him, when he's with me and when he's not.

Leni reaches for the radio and turns it on. "You know, while we're in Venice Beach, there's this thrift store I love."

I don't feel much like shopping, but there's nowhere I need to be.

Jagged Lovely, the thrift store, is large enough to hold maybe ten people. The woman inside greets us with a warm wave before returning to stock merchandise.

Leni makes a beeline for the dresses, and I tag along.

"You must need something," she prompts without looking up.

"I have my brother's wedding to go to in a couple of weeks."

"And you don't have a dress?" She grins. "You sure aren't like the usual ones."

"The usual what? Women Harrison hangs out with?"

She doesn't answer, but her hand flips through the hangers with reverence. She stops on a soft aqua cocktail dress with a white lace overlay. It's vintage and beautiful.

"What about this?"

"Um. Yeah, it might be long on you—"

"I meant for you."

I hold it up, surprised. It is beautiful. More delicate than something I'd normally choose.

"We have someone in house that does alterations," the woman working calls over.

"Thanks." I shove a hand through my hair. "I could try it on."

"You do that."

When I head toward the single changeroom stall in the back, I'm regretting the move. So much for Leni telling me about Harrison.

But as I strip out of my street clothes and start to tug the dress over my head, her voice drifts into the stall.

"There was this amazing thrift store back in college. I still have clothes from it today." She laughs. "Not sure how it stayed in business when everyone in that town was flush. Me, on the other hand? I was there on a mashup of scholarships and student loans."

My hands still after I tug the fabric down around my hips, facing away from the mirror. "That's when you met Harrison."

"Yep. He was the Richie Rich type. Add in that accent... whew. You can bet all the Park Avenue princesses wanted a piece of him."

I grin as I reach for the zipper.

"He indulged them. But no one caught his attention long enough to stick. He was smart, serious about his studies as a matter of pride even though he didn't have to be. That's how we got to be friends. I had this crappy basement apartment in town, so I practically lived at the library. He spent his share of time there too—I think because people didn't bother him."

I snort, enjoying the idea of a twenty-year-old Harrison King having to hide out to avoid unwanted attention.

"We were teamed up for a project for business school. Once he realized I was legit and I got over the idea that he was just like the others, we got to be friends. After graduation, I started working in PR in New York. It was my dream job, and I was going to pay off the massive student loans. But the man in charge of the agency—the same one who hired me six months before on the strength of my portfolio—fired me and took my ideas. I had no money and no options."

My chest tightens at the thought. "You called Harrison."

"No, he called me. He'd been keeping tabs and somehow heard what happened. He offered me a job running his first club. At first, I was too proud to take it. But when he assured me it wasn't just running a club, that he wanted to build an empire and he needed someone he trusted to help, I said yes."

"You're saying Harrison doesn't care where you come from."

"No. I'm saying he does."

I turn toward the mirror, and my breath sticks in my throat.

"Well?" Leni demands. "Is it on?"

She yanks on the curtain without waiting for me to respond.

"Damn, Rae," she whistles, inspecting me from head to toe. "I'm two for two today."

"It's a little loose here..." I pinch the back.

"You heard the woman. You can get it taken in. Problem solved."

After I change out of the dress and make arrangements for purchasing and alterations, Leni says, "I assume you're taking the boss to this wedding?"

"We haven't talked about it."

Miami was a big step for us, and I want to bask in the enjoyment of that before taking another crazy leap.

"Which is Raegan for 'I haven't given him a chance,'" she calls as we head back outside.

"Are you pissed or something?" I demand as I follow her up the sidewalk.

"I'm protective," she tosses. "I won't let anything bad happen on my watch."

I pull up a few feet from where the car is parked. "You're worried I'm going to hurt Harrison?"

Her sigh makes me feel as if I've missed something entirely.

She turns, leaning a tanned arm on the roof of the Jetta. She surveys me as if she's a teacher trying to decide if I'm worth the effort of educating.

"Before you left Ibiza, he did something big for you. I shouldn't even talk about it."

"Well, now you have to tell me."

Her expression says she doesn't have to tell me

shit. But I stare her down, and finally she relents.

"Christian made him an offer that would let him get La Mer. But he'd have to give you up to do it."

Shock rises up, twisting my stomach.

Harrison had a chance at winning the club he's always dreamed of, and he gave it up for me.

"He said no," Leni says, interrupting my thoughts.

The wind whips at my hair, and I brush it out of my face with unsteady fingers.

It doesn't make sense. None of it does.

I shake my head. "What kind of deal would even require—"

"It doesn't matter. There's nothing else to say," she says, her voice rising, "except that he said no."

Harrison

"Bank. Wasteland. Knot. But with a K," I add, disgusted.

Leni laughs from across the office in the future

club. "That's all marketing sent over for names?"

"The others are worse."

"If it doesn't sound like a place people want to go, no one will come."

It's been a week and a half since Miami, and we're making progress on the venue. The floors are coming together, and the walls are nearly complete.

With Rae and Leni's help, we've gotten most of the equipment sorted from the other club.

Of course, there's still the major problem of having this place rezoned.

My phone rings with a familiar number, and I hit Accept. "Leni's here too," I say by way of an answer.

"We should talk privately," comes my finance lead's voice over the speakerphone.

"You can say whatever you have to in front of her." But I rise and cross to the door, shutting it to keep out any ears from the other side.

He still hesitates. "Mischa's escalating. Buying more aggressively, a new club in Tokyo and one in Milan. Our intel doesn't show any major upgrades or changes to his venues, so we don't know where he's getting the capital—"

"From scaling his drug operations."

The words hang in the air.

If he has enough free cash to finance that, it's a bad sign for my planned acquisition of La Mer. My investigators are working around the clock on finding the evidence Christian wants, but I need it fast.

"How much can we afford to offer Geroux for La Mer?"

He names a number.

"I need more." I can't have Mischa blinding Christian with money, possibly making the old man succumb to greed when I need him to remember his honor.

He pauses, seeming to consider. "I could see about refinancing a couple of lease agreements. Find another five million. But's a short-term option at best."

"Do it. And stop Mischa from buying anything else in the interim."

"Stop him?" he echoes.

"Red tape," I reply, thinking of my own situation. "Miles deep. I want him focused on his problems, not on La Mer."

"If you're using short-term financing," Leni comments after I hang up, "making this new club a success is more important than ever."

And we're still waiting on a bloody hearing.

"It sucks that you have to play fair and Mischa doesn't..." She makes a face. "If it were Mischa waiting on an approval, Zachary would be hanging by his toes in a basement somewhere."

"On the contrary. Much can be achieved through reasonableness. What success requires is knowing when each is called for."

She watches as I place a call to the man who's causing my headaches—my stateside ones, at least.

"Zachary. Harrison King."

"To what do I owe the pleasure?" His tone is guarded.

"I have box seats to... a Lakers game," I decide on impulse.

But Leni waves her hands, shaking her head, and I frown.

"Ah, opening night. In—"

She mouths a word.

"—October. I understand you enjoy sports."

The quick investigation done by one of my staff says so.

"I couldn't accept them. I avoid all possibility of impropriety."

"I see. And the courtside seats to the Masters

tennis tournament in Palm Desert this spring. Those are public sector seats?"

Leni throws up her hands. Evidently, she's not impressed with my idea of reasonableness.

"Family friend," he says at last, his voice perceptibly cooler after my veiled threat. "Now, I don't know what you're implying, but if you'll excuse me—"

"I'm implying that we understand one another."

Some people can be bought. Others are persuaded by shows of strength, and by threats.

Neither will work with Whelan. Or at least, he's unwilling to be seen as being bought.

I'm not surprised given my research also suggested he comes from a moneyed family, but it's irritating nonetheless.

So, I change approaches.

"We're both men with significant influence."

My influence is far greater than his, but this is a negotiation, not a pissing contest. The reality is, he can make my life difficult. Which I don't want.

"You have a city to run and decisions to make as to its future. I respect a man who can't be distracted from his core mandate. I respect that more than you know. I'm committed to this investment, Zachary. The sooner we can get this queued up, the sooner we can make a toast to our respective futures and continue with our important work."

He's silent a long time. "I'll have our scheduler get it on the books. She'll follow up in the next day or two."

I hang up, grimly triumphant as a delivery arrives. Leni watches, obviously curious, as I open the garment bag and laugh.

"Jeans. Is this a joke?" she asks.

I grab the note from around the hanger.

Don't say I never bought you anything. Rae.

"No. It appears she's quite serious." My lips twitch.

We've been spending more time together. Since she and Leni went to negotiate the deal on our equipment with Blaze, she's stayed over at my condo twice, though she contended it was only because I let her have her preferred side of the bed.

The past few days, she's been traveling, busting her ass to make up more ground on the Wild Fest fan vote list. She's a powerhouse, and I dare anyone to try to keep her from something when she's made up her mind.

I've been aching without her.

So, when she proposed our plans for this evening, it felt like a step forward.

"We're going to a concert tonight," I tell Leni as I shuffle through the papers on the desk, tossing the list of potential names in the recycling bin where it belongs. "Tyler Adams's final show in Denver."

Leni sighs. "Well, fuck. You are in love with her."

I can't stop the way my chest tightens at the word. "Because I'm taking a beautiful woman to a concert?"

"No, because you're planning to wear those to do it." Her smile fades. "Your final year of college, before your parents died, you were ready to walk away from the family business."

"I was going to take my trust fund, move to some island, start a small tourist business to keep me busy, and never come back."

It sounds foolish now. Not only because that life wouldn't have sustained me, but because I was a naïve child who had no idea what the future held.

When my parents died, it hit me. The guilt. The emptiness. My responsibilities.

Now, I'm at the helm of a massive company. One that will expand until I crush the man who took this business and made it the kind of personal he can never take back.

"I'm still glad to see you doing something like this," Leni goes on, nodding toward me. "Even if those clothes will melt off your skin."

I shift out of my seat and cross to the door, lifting the garment bag off the hook on the back. "I'm not the devil, just a man who likes suits," I gripe.

But Leni's right. This matters even more than I figured. To Raegan and me, but also because the world will see us.

After our date on the beach with tacos, my PR firm emailed a number of photographs paparazzi took of the two of us.

I told them to buy the images. I didn't want anything scaring Reagan off when I was trying to convince her to spend time with me.

Now, I feel my pocket for the outline beneath. The box burns a hole in my clothing.

Soon enough, everyone will know what she means to me.

"Leni." I pause halfway out the door. "Have security lined up for Raegan. Starting tomorrow."

15

RAE

Rae: Sorry, traffic's a bitch. Be there in 15. Save me some whisky.

I'm late to meet Harrison at LAX to fly to Denver for Tyler's concert.

Harrison's going to be pissed. I get that it's a private plane and he won't be leaving without me, but still. He's used to things running a certain way, and he was the one who insisted on providing the transportation when I asked him about tonight.

So, when he texts me a picture of a drink, I nearly drop my phone.

. . .

Harrison: No promises. :)

Rae: Did you just smiley-face me? Who the fuck are you?

The limo pulls right up to the runway when I arrive, and I shift out with a single bag in tow. My boots click on the metal steps, echoing off the body of the plane. In the distance, others land and take off, but this section of LAX is quiet.

"Traffic was murder..." I say as I step into the private plane.

Harrison looks up from his phone. His mouth is pursed, brows pulled together on his handsome face. He's wearing the reading glasses I got him, but it's the way he's dressed that has me pulling up.

His windowpane button-down shirt is a blue that matches his eyes. The dark denim underneath clings to his strong thighs.

"Damn," I breathe. "I didn't think you'd actually wear it."

"In that case, I have a suit to change into." But he motions me over, and I drop my bag on the floor before sinking onto his lap.

"Quick, tell me you want me." My murmur is barely audible as the plane engine starts.

Harrison's pale lashes jerk as he looks between my eyes and my mouth. "I'm wearing denim. There's no greater evidence."

I grin and press my lips to his. One arm bands around my hips, pulling me closer, while his other hand angles my mouth against his so he can invade me with his tongue.

I used to chafe at the possessiveness, but it's growing on me.

Since Miami, we've been getting closer. We haven't revisited the conversation after my show, but knowing he knows what happened to me means one less thing between us.

Our time together is addictive. I don't need an excuse to see him. All I have to do is text him and we make plans. This man, the ruthless billionaire I used to hate, is a phone call away to share a joke, run an idea by. He makes me coffee before I'm awake, and even watched South Park with me for an entire evening when I didn't feel like going out.

The sex hasn't slowed down either. I take back my comments about age doing things to a man's endurance. He's relentless.

In bed, he takes me apart with his skilled

hands and mouth. His body is a finely tuned machine, hard planes and smooth muscles that know exactly how to make me split open.

And though I'm no porn star and don't play one on TV, you'd never know it by the way he looks at me, the sounds he makes when I'm touching him.

We haven't defined it, but it's so much more than casual. Not that anything with him has ever felt casual, but if there was any doubt, I'm pretty sure we blew past it the second I walked in on his stubborn ass sleeping on my couch in Miami, his rangy form contorted to fit the furniture because he refused to leave me.

Now, Harrison's lips slant deliciously across mine, sending waves of desire down my spine that settle into a sweet ache between my thighs, and I ignore that part of me.

He pulls back an inch. "As much as I'd like to continue this, we have to go. And to do it, you need to sit there."

I look at the leather seat over my shoulder. "Unfortunate."

But I comply, fastening my seatbelt as the plane prepares to take off.

"I can't believe you've never been to Red

Rocks," I say after settling in. "One of the world's greatest outdoor venues."

"I'm glad you can show it to me," he says. "Thank you. For inviting me."

Warmth floods me, has me looking away. "In fairness, we are taking your ride." I gesture to the plane.

"I'm serious. When was the last time you invited someone to join you and your friends?"

My instinct is to say it's not a big deal or deny the fact that I think about him all the time, that I naturally look to include him, and when I'm deciding what to do, I automatically check his schedule.

"Never," I admit.

The vulnerability creeps up. Since Miami, I've felt it more than once. Normally, it makes me shut down, but I'm learning to live with it.

There've been no games except the kind we're both on board for. I've never dated a man who's so direct about what he wants.

Although he still has an irritating habit of expecting he'll get it.

The plane takes off, and we stick to safe subjects for the majority of the two-and-a-half-hour flight.

"Your hard work this week is paying off." He holds out his phone, and I glance at the screen.

My brows lift. "Lucky number seven. Moving up in the world."

"You have two more weeks before they announce the fan vote. Any plans during that time?"

"It's a secret."

"Come on."

"It involves leather and a bullwhip and a video shoot on top of the Wynn hotel in Vegas."

"One, I don't believe you. And two"—his eyes darken—"if you ever do that, I swear to god I'll be the only one to see it."

I grin, because I've never dressed solely to provoke a man's reaction, but now I'm tempted. "How was your day?"

"You wouldn't believe what marketing is coming up with for the club's name."

"You should name it yourself. It's your crown jewel, after all."

"This club is regular business. The goal is still La Mer," he corrects. "Did I tell you my parents met there? In the early eighties. They fell in love in a single summer."

My chest aches at the longing in his voice. "You miss them."

"All the fucking time," he admits.

I still haven't figured out what Leni meant about Harrison giving up a chance at La Mer to be with me. Now, I wet my lips. "Back in Ibiza, it seemed you were close to a deal with Christian. Why couldn't you get it done then?"

He rests his head in one hand, studying me. "The price was too steep."

He's not telling me everything. I still don't know why he was willing to take that chance on me.

"No more talk of that," he says, picking up on my mood shift. "Let's discuss something pleasant. Like this wedding you're going to."

"My brother and I haven't spoken much in years. Things were tense around the time of...you know." I wave a hand in the air.

"But you've decided to go to his wedding."

I blow out a breath. "Seems that way. I ordered a dress."

"Show me."

I pull up a selfie on my phone that I snapped at the store.

"You'll be stunning in it."

"It cost forty-three dollars," I say proudly.

He flinches, as if personally wounded by the bargain I scored. "I'd like to go with you."

I shift in my seat. "Harrison, I like the dates we've been on. But this is different. It's family."

"Are you ashamed of me or of you?"

He holds out my phone and I struggle for words.

"It's not shame. It's more like... blame," I decide, rolling the word over on my tongue. "I blame them."

I've never said it out loud, but it's true.

I blame them for not having my back when they should have.

"May I give you some advice?" he murmurs, and I sigh.

"Is it something I don't want to hear?"

"Probably. Get even or get over it. If you don't, it will rot you."

I take the phone back and glance at the dress before clicking it off.

"Isn't that what's happening between you and Mischa?"

Harrison steeples his hands, surveying me with sudden intensity. "It's not the same. Did I tell you

Ivanov tried to recruit me when we were still in school?"

"Recruit you to what?" The metallic taste in my throat makes me swallow.

"His family business. Drugs, not clubs. I'd spent time with his parents over the years, and they knew I had the skills to take their business to the next level. I said no. Mischa tried to convince me."

My stomach tightens, and I feel my gaze drag down to where the scars sit on his chest under the shirt. "What did he do?"

"Everything he could. But in the end, I sent him back to his parents with his tail between their legs. What they did to him for failing?" He shakes his head. "That I don't know."

"He wants to beat you as much as you want to beat him," I realize.

"More," he says quietly. "I ruined his relationship with his parents. He killed mine. Neither of us will stop until one of us wins."

"You mean La Mer," I say, needing him to confirm it because this shit is taking on a scarier dimension than I expected.

He hesitates a beat. "Yes."

Damned men with their egos and war games.

"No matter who buys it, it'll still be Christian's baby," I point out. "This club in Burbank is yours. It will have your fingerprints all over it. Isn't it more of an accomplishment to create something from scratch than just to conquer what someone else built?"

His eyes glint with appreciation. "I suppose we'll find out."

When we arrive, a limo takes us from the tarmac straight to Red Rocks. Security gets us IDs and helps us meet up with Annie, Elle, Beck, and another woman in a VIP section. In addition, there's Annie's dad, Jax, and his wife, Haley.

Beck nods when he spots me. "Can't believe you're not passed out after the way we worked you over today."

"I'm going to sleep well tonight," I toss back.

Harrison's hand is on my hip. "Care to tell me what's going on?"

I hook a finger in the front pocket of his jeans, enjoying his irritated expression. "Nope."

On my way back from the bathroom, security is holding back a young woman.

"Little Queen, right? I'm a huge fan."

Normally, I would tense up at someone recognizing me out of costume, but I nod at security to let her through. "What's your name?"

"Amber. And I want to be a DJ. You're seriously my hero. I've been working on music for a few years, but it's nowhere near as good as yours. I wish I knew how to make it better." She flushes, looking embarrassed. "School's hard, and the music helps me stay focused. I shouldn't be telling you all this, but I'm nervous."

"It's cool. Music helped me get through shit too. Tell you what—send me something. We can talk about it."

I give her my email, and she clutches her phone to her chest. "Thank you."

When I get back to our booth, Harrison tugs me against his side. "Friend of yours?"

"A fan who wanted some advice about producing. I told her we'd talk."

The look in his eyes contains so many emotions—admiration, respect, something more than both.

"I recorded a set poolside at Beck's today," I blurt. I've busted my ass playing five shows in the last six nights, but I need to do more. "That's why I was late. His crew filmed it for his show, and it's going to drop in a couple of weeks. But we arranged for me to preview it on my feed and push the fan vote. Hopefully, it'll be enough to put me over the top."

His eyes shine. "You're brilliant."

The concert is spectacular, an orgy of music and lights and the energy of the crowd building and diffusing in that magical way only an outdoor venue seems to make possible.

For his part, Tyler's incredible. Annie watches with so much emotion and adoration it makes my chest hurt. I glance over at Harrison, his strong profile, and wonder if he watches me the same way.

After the show, we head backstage to hang with Tyler, celebrating with our friends.

By the end of the evening, we head back to our hotel. I'm thinking about Harrison's words from earlier about blame and revenge.

"Do you ever wonder how your life would be different if your parents hadn't died?" I ask in the back seat of the limo.

"Yes. I would be avoiding all responsibility. I would be the man the tabloids make me out to be, careless and unfeeling. Except the irony is the tabloids would no longer care because I wouldn't matter."

"It's funny how the worst things in our life give us a reason to do better."

His gaze locks on mine. "Sometimes I'm not sure. I've never much thought about what I'll do after claiming La Mer and burying Mischa."

I cock my head. "Well. You'll have more time to watch *GBBO*."

He snorts. "And after that?"

"You can catch up on *South Park*. There are a lot of seasons. Hundreds of episodes of social commentary and crass jokes that will make you do this."

I reach over and press one of his brows up his forehead.

He's laughing, and the idea of him sitting through my favorite episodes has me grinning too.

"I know what it is to want justice for your past," I say once we've recovered. "But if the price is your future? It's not worth it. You can start over."

He tugs me toward him.

"You're too young to be this wise," he murmurs, capturing me with his eyes as much as his hold.

I've never felt the way I feel under the intensity of his study. The strong, commanding man is still there in his handsome face, sharp brows, and nose and jaw.

"This thing between us, Raegan. I didn't plan on it."

My brows shoot up. "Oh, and you think I did? You think I tracked you down at Tyler and Annie's wedding, tanked my career, followed you to Ibiza to have a shot with you?"

He frowns but doesn't answer. Only reaches into his pocket and produces a square red box with gold writing on top. *Cartier.*

Nerves grip me. It's clearly not a ring, and I can't picture him proposing since he said he never would again, but it's jewelry.

As outrageous as the diamond headphones were, I justified that they were related to my work, what I was doing with him.

Whatever's in that box is about us.

There's nothing to hide behind.

"Open it."

"I don't want to."

He taps a foot, impatient. "It won't bite."

My hands shake a little as I open the case, and I'm accosted with the sheen of gold. The bracelet is a dazzling circle, wide as three of my fingers.

"A cuff?"

"Figured it was more your style than a tennis bracelet."

The bracelet is simple and elegant. Edgy too. It would take on the style of anything you wore with it while maintaining its own classic perfection.

When I lift it from the case, it's heavier than I expect.

"Does it come with a lock and key? I assume this is to keep me from running away again."

He doesn't laugh. "It's to tell you *I'm* not leaving."

I shift in my seat, fidgeting as I look away. "The most expensive gift I've ever gotten was from my parents after..." I trail off, shaking my head. "Are you asking me to be your girlfriend?"

Harrison's eyes grow flinty, and the words hang between us long enough I feel like a fool.

Maybe I misread this. He's been spending a lot of time with me, but now a lump rises up my throat at the idea that he's not in this the way I thought. Jealousy. Insecurity. One ugly emotion after the other, and I can't shove them away fast enough.

I'm the girl who didn't want commitment. And now, suddenly, I do?

I turn away, but he plants his hands on either side of my hips.

"Labels like 'boyfriend' and 'girlfriend' aren't for people like us." My chest tightens, twists, but he plows on. "We live at the edge of success and failure. Where falling down causes more than a scratch. I see you. You might be young, but I know you. When I fuck up, it impacts thousands of people. When you fall, they feel it. I will be with you when you do.

"There's a name for that. It's not 'girlfriend.'"

I turn the bracelet in my fingers, and my gaze lands on the inscription.

My Queen.

My heart stops.

It's not about me or about him. It's about us. The magic that happens when we're together.

The way I feel when I'm around him.

I was afraid the feeling was fragile or that I'd be fragile if I leaned on it. But I realize it's not. And I'm not.

"I hoped you'd like it." There's uncertainty in his voice. "If not, I—"

I press a finger against his lips. "Put it on me."

16

RAE

*T*he slippery feeling on my skin won't go away.

My eyes blink open. There's a hint of the sun coming through the curtains in our hotel room, but the clock says it's nine.

Harrison is asleep next to me—unusual for him. I steal the chance to watch him, his aristocratic nose, firm mouth, thick lashes. Golden hair falls over his forehead, his firm chest rising and falling with his breath. The scar he'll never erase, the one that seems carved into his brain as much as it's carved into his body.

I'm starting to see the power of forgiving your past while it feels he's going deeper into his. The worry he carries worries me, for him and for us.

I play with the bracelet still on my wrist, glinting defiantly even in the dull light. It's nothing I would ever buy myself, but the more I look at it, the more I see me in it—the inscription, which makes my stomach quiver with an emotion I can't name out loud, but also the cuff. It's not classic jewelry, and it's even more special for it.

He asked me to keep it on after we got back.

Since we returned to the hotel, it's the only thing I've kept on.

Now, my body is heavy and languid in the best way, as it always is after a long night with him.

My phone vibrates on the nightstand, and I pick it up.

Beck: Can you check on the house? I need to fuck off for a couple of days.

I'm not the kind of person to overthink other peoples' internal worlds, but when I set down the phone, I can't kick the feeling of concern.

The carpet is soft under my bare feet as I shift out of bed and pad naked into the living room, pulling the door closed behind me.

"Yeah," Beck answers raggedly on the second ring.

"What's wrong?" I ask under my breath, hoping I don't wake Harrison in the other room.

"We're done. I overheard my supposed girlfriend last night saying she was dating me to get on the show and help her own career."

My ribs ache. "No. I thought you guys were good."

"Guess you can't change someone's heart, you know? She wanted me, but she wanted fame more. The fucked-up thing is I would've given it to her if she'd asked."

I squeeze my eyes shut against the hurt in his voice. "Where are you now?"

"The airport. About to get on a plane for a change of scenery. Shooting's done for the drama, but I can't even think about *Being Beck* right now. If I go on camera trying to live my life, I'm gonna break down. My producer would say the fans'll be down with it, but he'll want to vilify the girl."

"It sounds like she deserves it."

"I'm not the guy to decide what people deserve."

Beck might be hurting now, but forgiving her

will let him move on. I wish the rest of us could learn the same.

"Don't leave LA," I say as I hear Harrison stirring in the other room. "We're flying back in a couple of hours. I'll meet you at your place this afternoon."

The bedroom door opens as I hang up.

"Good morning," I tell Harrison, who looks rumpled and sexy as fuck. His hair is a mess, his blue eyes at half-mast. He's naked except for black boxer briefs, the fabric stretched thanks to a very discernable erection, and every muscle and plane of his gorgeous body is on display. My throat dries.

"It is. But we could take a shower and make it better." His eyes darken as he takes me in, and I'm already wet from his indecently slow inspection.

He wraps both arms around me, the heat of his skin feeling like home.

I hold up my wrist. "Is gold shower-proof?"

"Let's find out."

"I want to. You have no idea how much." He rubs his erection between my thighs, which only makes me groan. "But I need to get back for Beck."

"I have an eight-figure investment burning cash until it's rezoned, and you don't see me sprinting onto the plane. Though perhaps I should bring you with me to the hearing. No doubt you could charm that prick Whelan and his zoning committee."

I stiffen. "Who?"

"Zachary Whelan. The head of the zoning commission."

There's not enough air in the room, and I pull out of his arms to get a glass of water from the bathroom.

Once I've drained it, I turn back to him.

"Harrison... I know Zach Whelan."

"From what?"

"He was a friend of Kian's growing up."

He crosses to me, folding me in his arms once more. My skin prickles with awareness even though my head is a million miles away.

"Then you *can* charm him." He curses. "Dammit, we should've figured this out sooner—"

"It's better I don't see him. And don't mention me to him."

"Tell me you didn't break his heart." Harrison smirks. "If I learn you slept with him, I'm going to have to kill the poor asshole, and then I'll never get my permit."

"I'm serious." My fingers dig into his muscled arms, and he frowns.

I don't think he's going to let it go, but finally he relents. "Well, we both have reasons to get back, but surely they can wait long enough for me to take you in the shower." Harrison's mouth descends to my neck. His teeth and lips send sparks along my nerve endings, making my body pull tight in arousal and distract from the dark thoughts in my head.

"Surely."

"What's in the bag? Weed?" Beck asks when I arrive that afternoon, a paper bag in my arms.

He peers in the top, eyebrows lifting. "Ice cream. Solid."

We take it to the living room, Beck grabbing two spoons from the kitchen on the way.

"You gonna paint my fingernails too?" he quips, sinking onto the couch.

"Don't hold your breath."

He peels off the top of the carton of fudge marshmallow and takes a bite. His low groan is half satisfaction, half longing. "That's good."

I turn on the TV and navigate to the channel I've memorized since spending more time with

Harrison.

"You want to watch soccer?" he scoffs. "You're a terrible wingwoman."

I say nothing, wait for play to end, and the cameras to zoom in on one of the players at the end of a sequence.

Beck shifts forward, frowning. "Yeah. Okay, sure." He reaches for another bite of ice cream. "Half a pint of this, I'll be nonverbal."

I take the carton from him and scoop a bite of my own. The rich flavors hit my tongue, and I groan.

Beck cuts a look at the screen, a low rumble of laughter escaping his chest. "Shit. That the kid from the boat?"

Ash brings the ball up the field, his expression tight with intensity.

"You have two years on him. Stop pretending it's a generation."

The camera zooms out as Ash passes the ball off, gets it back. Then with a lightning-fast move, he redirects it toward the goal.

There's no chance. He's too fast, the ball slicing through the air.

The goaltender dives...

And suddenly, a defenseman comes out of nowhere to deflect the ball.

Ash's handsome face is anguished, the camera showing him tug on his hair before running back up the field the other way.

The commentators speak overtop of the broadcast, stats I don't fully understand appearing on a digital graphic on one side of the screen. Apparently, it's been an up-and-down season for one of the sport's most promising talents.

"Looks like he's having a rougher year than I thought."

Beck's gaze narrows on the TV. "He doesn't know what the fuck to do with himself. He doesn't know who he is."

"You got all that from meeting him once and seeing him on TV?"

"How could anyone not get that?" Beck chuckles. "Things must be going well if you're DVR'ing the little bro's games." The look on his face tells me he won't put up with me holding back on account of his broken heart or for any other reason.

"He gave me this bracelet."

I hold out my wrist, and Beck grins. "I'm glad he's taken his head out of his ass long enough to know you're the real deal. That'll go with the dress you ordered."

He points at a garment bag in the living room that I somehow missed. I shift off the couch and unzip the bag.

"All you need is a billionaire on the other arm to match," Beck says.

"Harrison's not coming."

"Why the fuck not?"

"I didn't invite him. Him being there would complicate things."

"Seems to me if you trust him, you should give him a shot with the family," Beck goes on. "The guy's heavy handed, sure, but he cares about you. I saw it when he crashed our dinner. If you're worried he'll go AWOL and interrogate Grandma over spinach puffs, tell him to stay in his lane or he won't get invited back."

"It's not my life I'm worried about him fucking up. If he talks to the wrong people...he's not going to like what he finds."

I thought Harrison knew my secrets, but this morning I learned there's one thing tying my past to the future he wants. The one he needs.

I won't put that future at risk, even if I have to hurt him to do it.

Before I can respond, there's a knock on the door. A huge guy with a buzzed head is on the step, dressed in a black suit and sunglasses. There's a handheld radio on his belt.

"Who are you?" I ask.

Those glasses slide down his face as he addresses me. "Security, ma'am."

"Whose security?"

"Yours."

17

HARRISON

"*Y*ou're still angry about the security," I say, surveying my girlfriend from the four-poster bed where I'm lying fully clothed. "That's why you won't let me come to this wedding."

"You arranged it without my knowledge or consent. Sent an armed meathead to Beck's door—"

"I would've thought he'd enjoy that."

Rae's quiet, even for her, industriously gathering her bag, lipstick, fussing with her hair in the mirror of our boutique hotel in Napa.

"That's beside the point. It's not why you're not coming to the wedding."

"Then what's the problem?"

She straightens, turning to look at me. She's beautiful, her blue dress hugging curves I dream about every second I'm not touching them. Her eyes are dark, lined to make them darker, her lips full and parted. Her hair falls in soft waves around her shoulders thanks to a curling iron she burnt herself on while she was finishing.

"You can't come because it's family and in public and a cesspool of emotions and damage, and I didn't ask for a plus one. Especially a plus one who's recognizable and infamous and going to draw attention like a magnet."

Frustration rises up. "So, I'm good enough to drive you up here but not to attend the ceremony."

"That's bullshit."

"Is it?" I cross to her and box her in against the dresser.

The wedding is at a vineyard. I drove with her and stayed over, thinking a night away would be refreshing.

I get that she RSVPed for one person weeks ago, but it feels as if she doesn't want me to know where she comes from.

"You knew who I was when we started this," I murmur. "Don't invite me in one moment and shut me out the next."

She steps into her heeled platforms, tossing her hair over one shoulder as she bends to fasten the straps.

"Inviting you in feels like inviting a circus," she says, still bent double. "I want you, but I can't take the monkeys today, Harrison."

Perhaps I should have anticipated her reaction. But I've rarely encountered a woman who didn't want to be with me, who didn't welcome all that came with it. Even my ex acted like she wanted it— until she didn't.

But there's a larger issue.

Rae's my girlfriend, as trite as the label is. That means I get to claim her as mine—in public when we're walking down the street and in private when she's panting beneath me. It also means I get to tease her. That she's the person I think of first when I run into a problem.

From the way she's been carrying tension since Colorado, the way she burnt herself with the styling tool she could use in her sleep, today is a problem.

But she's not fucking confiding in me, and that eats me alive. She's using this event as an excuse not to let me in. She can't shut me out whenever it's convenient, whenever something triggers her to raise the walls she's spent years carefully building.

"There's a brave woman I can't stop thinking about," I bite out. "You're not acting like her."

She straightens, eyes wide with shock. It's the first sign I've landed a blow. "You should drive back to LA. I'll get my own ride back."

We go downstairs in silence and wait while the valet brings the car around.

When she drops into the passenger seat, her handbag falls on the floor. As she fishes under the seat to retrieve it, I put the car in gear, not bothering to help.

The moment we pull up the long driveway of the vineyard and I park in front, she shifts out and shuts the door.

The car is too quiet as I head back to the highway, so I crank the satellite radio. My knuckles are white on the wheel.

I came to LA for business. To put Mischa in the ground, professionally speaking. Instead, all I can think of is the woman I left twenty miles back.

Being this consumed by another person isn't healthy, but I don't know how to change it or even if I want to. I've never had someone this tightly linked to my work and life.

A ringing sounds from the passenger seat.

What the…?

As the ringing cuts out, I pull over and reach under the seat.

Her phone.

She must have dropped it when she dropped her bag. She'll almost certainly need it.

I turn the car around.

Rae

There's a rule that weddings should be happy. A day to reminisce about times past, dream of the future.

But with Callie at my side, my small talk with relatives and family friends is loaded.

"I haven't seen you in forever. What are you doing?" is the inevitable question.

"I work in the music industry."

In most crowds, that would inspire more questions, but with my family, that's usually enough to shut people down. It's better to be in law or medicine or politics.

We claim seats in the back, and I open my clutch to text Harrison and say I'm sorry for what happened earlier. He was being unreasonable, but his intuition wasn't wrong.

I've been dreading this day, and I have been keeping him at a distance.

Still, I wish Harrison was with me now—not as protection but because I enjoy his company. The vineyard makes me wonder whether he'd like it or scoff at the natural flowers, which Callie told me cost thousands. If, when pressed, he'd say something like, "If you're going to spend on flowers, make it look like you did."

"What's wrong?" my cousin asks when I curse.

"My phone is missing. Maybe I dropped it." I stand and dash up the aisle to the main building but run smack into a tuxedo-clad form on the way. I look up to see my brother's equally surprised face. "Kian!"

"Rae. Shit, it's good to see you."

"You look great. I haven't seen you in anything other than scrubs in years."

"I haven't seen you in anything in years," he points out. "You haven't come home."

"I know." Loaded tension settles between us, and I swallow hard.

"It's okay," he says before I can find words. "I forgive you."

I lift a brow. "*You* forgive *me*?"

"Yeah. I mean, when you left for arts school and never came back to visit, even when you worked in LA, I took it personally. But I'm your big brother, and I know I was caught up in my own shit with med school. So, I forgive you. It's that easy."

Suddenly, the music starts. As I look around, I'm thinking of all the good times we had as kids, and the heavy stuff falls away.

"This is a big day," I murmur.

"Start of forever," he agrees, looking nervous for the first time I can remember. "I keep thinking she'll come to her senses and say no. Like the officiant will say, 'Do you?' and she'll respond, 'Fuck this noise. I'm out.' I never thought I'd be getting married. But life changes you, right?"

My throat tightens as I nod. "You have your something old, new, borrowed, and blue?"

"Think that's a bride thing, sis."

I tear a tiny piece of lace off the overlay hem of

my dress. "Here. It's repurposed vintage and borrowed. Just in case."

His eyes soften, and he pulls me in for a hug.

When Kian heads to the altar to take his place, I remember my missing phone.

It's too late to go look for it before the start of the ceremony.

I huff out a breath as I slump back in my seat.

"Did you see Kian?" Callie asks when I sink back into my chair.

"He looks good. Happy."

She squeezes my hand. "Are you happy?"

"I will be," I say.

There's a man I care about, and the second I get back to LA, I'll tell him how badly I wished he'd been by my side today.

The procession music begins, and the first couple comes down the aisle. My attention lingers on the bridesmaid's dress. The hem kisses the ground as she walks.

"Pretty sure I heard them fucking in the cellar when I got here," Callie comments, and I swallow a laugh.

The second couple starts, but this time, all I can see is the back of the groomsman's suit. Every muscle in me stiffens.

"What's wrong—oh, shit." Callie grabs for my hand.

I can't look away.

"I didn't think he and Kian were still friends. I didn't know he'd be here..." Callie's furious whisper echoes in my ears, and I feel her turn toward me. "Did you?"

There's no way I can answer.

Because when the couple reaches the front and the groomsman turns, I feel as if I've been shot in the stomach.

18

HARRISON

I park at the end of the row, not bothering with the valet.

The ceremony is over—the bride and groom are outside, taking pictures. Guests mill about, cocktails in hand. I cross the green expanse toward the vines and the bar, Rae's phone in my grip.

None of the faces are hers.

A pair of women glances toward me, and their attention lingers as they freeze. Then one of the women grabs another passing by, drawing her in and whispering.

But I press forward toward the bar, where my gaze catches on a familiar profile. "Whelan."

Zachary turns, and the man who holds my club's future in his hands straightens his tailored suit. "Harrison." His mouth curves. "And here I thought putting you on the calendar for this week would get you off my back."

I extend a hand, and he takes it.

"What are you doing here?" I ask.

"Friend of the groom."

"Right. I recall my girlfriend saying she knew you. Raegan Madani," I go on as I look past him, searching for her amidst the crowd.

When I turn back to the man in front of me, he's transformed.

"This some kind of joke?" His voice is low, his lips thinning into a line.

I don't answer. I'm too busy trying to figure out what could've happened to set him off in the space of a single breath.

Not even a breath. A *name*.

Rae's name.

My body tenses. There's something I'm missing, a piece just out of reach.

"Not a joke." I'm bluffing but match his low tone.

I didn't like this man the first time I met him, and that emotion is quickly seeping toward repulsion as he looks around furtively.

"Anything that happened was a long time ago, and it was between us."

What the fuck?

"You've been around," he goes on. "You know how it is. In college, you like to drink, experiment. Girls see an older guy they want..." He wets his lips. "It's how rumors get started."

The vineyard falls away, the world receding down to a point that's Zachary, his reddening face and shifting eyes and expensive tux with the boutonnière.

When I speak, each word is soft. "Ah, yes. Those rumors."

Sweat beads on his face. "It was Kian's party." His throat bobs. "She shouldn't have even been there."

In Miami, she said started making music in high school after she was raped, that her parents began fighting after something disrupted their family, ended up divorcing.

The way she doesn't rely on anyone to look out for her. The identity she forged, the one that makes it easier for her to be free, to separate herself from someone who doesn't have fears...

That's why she didn't want me here today. She knew he would be, or could be.

Zachary Whelan isn't only the man responsible for the fate of my club.

He's the man who raped my girlfriend.

People are watching us, recognizing me.

I don't care. I step closer, fisting his lapel and leaning in until his awful cologne hits my nostrils.

"Say another word," I mutter, "and I will break one of these wine bottles and castrate you in front of the bride and groom."

His eyes widen in shock.

But before I can rip Whelan to shreds, a woman's voice calls my name.

"Harrison!"

I turn, but it's not my girlfriend. Though she's physically similar and around the same age, this woman is taller, wearing a different dress, and the expression on her face is a warning as she looks between me and Whelan.

"Callie," I guess, and she nods. "I'm in the middle of—"

"I can't find Rae anywhere."

Rae

The cellar's damp but comforting. Quiet and far enough from the rest of the party that no one will find me.

Except footsteps have me tensing, and dress shoes appear on the stairs.

I made it through the ceremony, focusing steadfastly on my brother and his beaming bride.

The moment it was done, before the recessional, I asked Callie to cover for me and snuck out.

I found my way down to a room with wine barrels and sank onto the floor. I don't have a watch, so I can't know how much time has passed.

The dress shoes' owner descends.

I thought I could handle seeing family and old friends. I didn't expect *he* would be here.

Making peace with your past is one thing. Sitting twenty feet from the man who assaulted you is a stretch.

When dark dress pants appear, followed by a belt and a pale blue shirt I personally picked out this morning, my chest eases.

The soft, yellow overhead light shines on Harrison's hair as he emerges into the cellar.

"You came back." My voice is rough.

He crosses the space between us and holds out something. "You left your phone in the car."

My fingers close around it, the case cool and familiar.

"I ran into Whelan upstairs."

Harrison's fists clench at his sides. He shifts onto a barrel near where I'm sitting, easing back to stretch his legs. There's a smudge of dirt on his pants, but if he's uncomfortable, he doesn't let on. "Why is the man who assaulted you at your brother's wedding?"

I swallow hard. "Kian didn't know. I blamed him still, which wasn't fair."

"What happened to you wasn't fair."

"But I can't control that. Forgiving my brother... I can do that."

Each breath is a little easier with him here.

"You didn't tell me it was Whelan because I need him to get the venue approved?"

I nod. "I didn't want you to lose the project over it."

With a heavy sigh, he shifts off the barrel and eases himself onto the dusty floor next to me. He's anything but relaxed, and he's obviously trying to fight whatever dark instincts are inside him.

After a moment's hesitation, I lean my head against his shoulder and breathe him in. "Did you kill him?"

"Not yet. Would you like to watch?"

My exhale is half laugh and half sob. He takes my phone and sets it on the floor, threading his fingers through mine.

We sit like that for minutes. Maybe longer.

Finally, the device buzzes with a message from Callie.

Callie: I don't know if you found your phone, but I'm not sure how else to find you. Where are you? Are you okay?

Callie: I lost track of you when the aunts cornered me after the ceremony. Did you bail?

Callie: Kian was looking for you, and I wasn't sure what to tell him.

.   .   .

Callie: I ran into Harrison, who's looking for you too. Keep an eye out for the beautiful blond man who looks like he's going to rain down hellfire.

My mouth twitches. I reluctantly pull my hand from Harrison's to type back. He caresses my knee as if unwilling to stop touching me.

I don't hate it.

Rae: I'm okay. I needed some space, but I'm with Harrison. Tell Kian he did great.

"What I said earlier about you not being brave today... I was wrong. You're the bravest woman I know."

Harrison's gaze locks with mine. In it is the compassion I didn't know I needed.

Back when it happened, I didn't have many people to talk to. The ones I did confide in made it seem like I put this problem on them. The ones I tried to hide it from acted as if my withdrawing from the activities I previously did was an act of selfishness.

Now, the man I care about is looking at me like there's nothing wrong with me.

More than that, like there's something admirable about me, in me.

My gaze drifts to one of the wine casks next to me. "Want to get drunk tonight?"

His lips tug up, his handsome face rueful as he rises to standing. He brushes the dirt off his pants before offering a hand. "After I drive us back to LA. I'll have the hotel sommelier bring us a selection."

I consider. "Maybe have him take the night off and we can raid the wine cellar."

"Done."

I grab his hand, and he tugs me up in one easy motion.

"Before you suggest laying charges, I've considered it," I say as I adjust my bag on my shoulder. "Not at first, but later. The statute of limitations is up, though, so I couldn't if I wanted to."

He exhales heavily, then pops the top button on his shirt as if he needs the air. "In that case, let's go home."

I don't argue with his choice of words.

19

HARRISON

*R*ae didn't protest when I brought her back to my place or when I fumbled with the kettle to make tea. In truth, I felt more shaken than she looked. We spent the evening watching *South Park*, half my brain trying to understand the statistical likelihood of a boy named Kenny being plagued by such obscure, violent threats week after week. The other half of my brain was simply grateful to have Raegan curled against my side.

The next morning, I look at her in my bed. My chest twists like there's a knot of muscle deep in my torso. She's too fucking young to have gone through what she has. Too brave for me to taunt her about being weak.

She will never go through it again and the man who hurt her will beg for a fate like Kenny's.

Leaving her in bed, I close the door before I pad barefoot out to the kitchen and start coffee. The smell might wake her, but I don't want my sounds to.

I ignore the dozens of notifications on my phone as I pull up her social profile, going right back to the post she never deleted, reaming me out this spring. I watch it again, emotions colliding in my chest.

Now I understand why she's so fixated on ensuring women are protected in clubs—mine or anyone else's. It's not only an issue that matters to her—it's one that shaped her.

It's shaped me through her.

I swipe a finger up the screen, and the feed scrolls, dozens of images. From Ibiza and since. Plus the live feed she did from Beck's last week, fresh and grinning.

Thanks to that, she's at number three on the Wild Fest fan vote.

I'm beyond proud of her.

The way she glows on stage. The way she tries. The way she'll fight for other people but hides her heart because she doesn't want it trampled.

The most recent photo is a poster for her gig in New York this week—her last push before the organizers decide. I can't attend thanks to an important meeting in London later this week.

I want to be there for her.

What I want more, though, is to kill the man who hurt her with my bare hands.

The hearing is scheduled for tomorrow. The fate of my club rests in the balance, but suddenly there's something even more important at stake.

I click out of social media and into my contacts list, dialing a number I rarely use.

———

"You don't need to handle this," Leni insists. "We have lawyers and petitioners who can do the heavy lifting."

Hearings are a place for the general public to trot out their objections and for officials and the committee to ask questions. They're not something I'd deign to participate in if it weren't important. And since the head of zoning is the man who raped my girlfriend, it's fucking important.

When I show up at the meeting, there's a modest crowd. My lawyers handle most of the conversation on my behalf. There are some ridiculous questions and pressures from a local interest group that make me sit up.

"Mr. King has a reputation for taking over clubs only to mismanage them. We don't want a large venue in our community."

"Those claims are unsubstantiated," my lawyer says.

"I have reports dating back years." He holds up a stack of papers, takes them over to the commission.

"Give me a copy," I demand.

The man does.

They're the usual "not in my backyard" allegations, plus some disturbingly short-sighted arguments aimed at dismantling our claims that the club will enhance the surrounding area.

"The committee will take this under consideration," Zachary concludes from the front. "We'll take a short recess before our next agenda item."

He gets up to use the washroom. I follow him in.

The man goes into a stall, and I wait at the sink, meeting his gaze in the mirror when he comes out to wash his hands.

"That was... disappointing," I say.

Another man starts to enter, but I cut him a look and he quickly reverses out the door.

"I told you. Interest groups are very active here."

A few days ago, I was convinced we could work together. He'd be one more bureaucrat I'd manage.

By Saturday afternoon, I realized that would never happen.

"You're from a good family," I start. "Political. Affluent. Elite golf course memberships. Old money. It must be nice to be so connected. To have kids. A wife."

"Ex-wife," he bites out.

"The divorce is before the courts. Do she and her lawyers know you raped a teenage girl?"

"You can't threaten me." He sneers, his confidence bolstered by the lawyer he dialed the second he left the wedding—the one who no doubt reminded him he was in the clear for whatever heinous acts he committed more than ten years ago.

"That's not why I'm here." I jerk on a paper towel, and two sheets tumble out.

"Then why?"

I toss him one sheet. "Because I needed to look in your eyes, but more than that, I needed you to look in mine." The second paper towel crumples into a ball under the pressure of my fist, and I toss it into the trash without taking of my gaze from the man before me. "You hurt someone I love. In the most repugnant, despicable way a man can hurt a woman."

The protectiveness I feel for her is different from anything I've ever experienced.

"God might absolve you of that sin." I lean in, savoring the fear edging into his eyes. "I will not."

20

RAE

Rae: How was it?

I text Harrison when the plane pulls up to the gate at La Guardia. I'll be in New York for a few days to see Annie and perform my final gig, but the timing meant I had to leave the same day as Harrison's meeting with the zoning commission.

Harrison: No bloodshed.

. . .

My chest unknots a degree, but I don't totally buy it.

Rae: I want a picture.

Moments later, the joke's on me because he sends through an image of of his chest, abs, and the trail of hair leading to the band on his boxer briefs.

I nearly drop the phone.

The woman next to me must be pushing seventy, and she makes a sound of appreciation. "Well done."

"Thanks." I swallow a laugh and type back.

Rae: Just getting off the plane. I'll call you later. My neighbor thinks you're hot.

I tuck the phone away to disembark.

I've got it bad. Since Kian's wedding, I'm falling even harder for him.

We're both on the go, and I don't know what

getting more serious means, but I miss Harrison when he's not around.

Uncharted territory. That's what this is.

Tomorrow is a huge gig that will decide Wild Fest, but I'm thinking about Harrison.

By the time I get into the hotel and get through some emails for the show tomorrow, it's late.

It's three hours earlier in LA, I remind myself as I hit his contact.

Harrison answers the video call on the second ring. "I was concerned my photo gave you a heart attack."

His gruff voice makes me grin.

"No, but the woman sitting next to me on the plane enjoyed it."

He cocks his head. "She single?"

"And at least seventy."

"Perfect."

"You're not," I remind him. "Single *or* seventy."

He laughs, and I notice his shirt, open at the front to expose a tantalizing glimpse of skin. I swallow.

"Why were you naked earlier?"

"Trying on some new suits." He's in motion the next second, flipping the camera to display half a dozen jackets.

"You're a clothes whore."

"I bought you something too." He flips the screen back, smirking. I'm curious what he got me, but he continues before I can ask. "I'm flying to London tomorrow for a few days. A few conversations with senior Echo staff."

"Oh." I'd almost forgotten he has work outside of LA because he's been here so much. "Did you get the approval for the club?"

The backboard of his bed appears as he shifts onto the mattress. "Not today. I have more urgent matters to attend to first. Mischa's been causing problems."

It always seems as if his vendetta trumps what he could create in the future.

"Are you ready to decimate the competition and claim the top spot in Wild Fest's fan vote tomorrow?"

I stop pacing and sink onto the couch, staring at my computer on the coffee table that contains the set I've worked and reworked. I make a face to hide the nerves. "I have a set. But nothing feels right." I pull up the track I was planning to open with, then click to another and another. I leave the third one running, turning down the volume so it throbs in the background as we continue talking.

"I've done some research on the crowd. The club sent me some demographics, and..."

He groans, and I trail off.

"My beautiful girlfriend is an exceptional producer who still doesn't understand what the people want."

"Which is?"

I frown at my Ableton software, wishing there was an answer that didn't rely on my own intuition.

"What I already have."

His voice lowers, and I flick my gaze back to the phone screen. His firm mouth is parted as he shifts back, eyes darkening.

The music pulses in the background like a dark metronome.

Awareness heats my blood, has my body taking notice.

"Set your phone down. Somewhere I can watch you."

A breath trembles out from between my lips. But I do it, glad to not have to make a decision for once today.

When the phone is propped against my computer, I lift a brow. "Anything else?"

His gaze takes me in, my pajama shorts and tank top, my messy hair around my shoulders.

"Lose the shirt."

I hesitate a beat before stripping it off.

I'm half a dozen feet from the window but on a high floor. It's unlikely anyone can see in, but I feel exposed anyway.

I've been naked in front of Harrison plenty of times, but this feels different. When his breath goes shallow, his gaze lingering on my lips, my shoulders, the curve of my breasts, the hard points of my nipples, I shiver.

"You're stunning, Raegan. If you knew half of what you did to me..."

A wave of light-headedness washes over me at the desire in his voice.

"Touch yourself. Let me see it."

My heart thuds in my chest, skipping at his request. It's a challenge, but more than that, it's a plea.

When I skim a hand up my stomach, over my breast, he exhales tightly.

I like that I have this much power over him.

That high urges me on. I pinch my nipple and squeeze the mound of flesh surrounding it, rewarded once by the sensations flooding through me and again by Harrison's groan.

"Fuck. You do this to them too, you know. You can't see it from the stage, but they want how you make them feel. More than that, they want who you are."

They want Little Queen, I correct in my mind. But it's hard to think with what we're doing. What I'm doing.

His hand slips out of the camera's view, and the visual glitches. I imagine his hand wrapped around his cock. Stroking.

If I asked to see it, would he let me?

But that's not what this is about, I realize as the track changes to another of my songs.

I rise from the couch and tug my shorts off, laying them on the cushion before I sit back down.

My hand goes back to my breast, the other one drifting down.

I slip it between my folds where I'm wet, and my head falls back on a silent moan.

"You like watching me?" I murmur, loving the flare of his nostrils, the rise and fall of his chest with shallow breaths.

"Almost as much as I like fucking you."

My laugh is low. I rub two fingers over my clit, gasping in surprise at how sensitive I am already.

I stroke myself, slow at first, half tempo. Any self-consciousness ebbs little by little as my music swells in the background. My man's ravenous expression and groans turn me on even more.

"The first time I knew you were going to be a problem was in Ibiza. You were rubbing your head because of tension headaches and planning your second set for Debajo. I'd just thrown out your meds and you were spitting venom and I kept wondering what you'd say if I laid you down on the kitchen table and ate you."

"I would've said less lip, more tongue," I tease.

His eyes flash with heat, and an emotion that makes my chest tighten.

Heat floods my skin as I dial up my strokes, my other hand slipping down my stomach to help as I arch, my head dropping back against the couch.

"Raegan, fuck."

He's agonized, but I'm enthralled. It's a spell I'm weaving on myself as much as one he's weaving on me.

It feels so good. Wild. Free.

I come on my own fingers, crying out as the

shockwaves start at my core and ripple through every part of me.

Moments later, I hear his hard groan.

I shut my eyes and imagine him coming on me, spilling over my body.

When we finish, my breath coming back to normal, he asks, "How do you feel?"

I crack my eyes open, my attention cutting from his handsome face and dilated pupils to my computer and the new track that started just moment ago.

I shift forward, biting my lip as I scan the screen. "I think I'm going to open with this."

"My ass is burning. You willingly do this?" I demand.

"Four times a week," Annie confirms as we grab our bags and head out of the studio barre class.

"Can't picture Tyler doing that to look good on stage."

"He doesn't have to. He's done four shows a week all summer. His ass is great."

"And you're moving back to LA in a few weeks?"

"Yup. He doesn't have family, and my dad's in Dallas. We always thought we'd come back east when Tyler's contract was up, but LA is growing on me and the winters bug him. I like the idea of raising kids in California."

I nod toward her stomach. "Find out if it's a boy or a girl?"

"I want to be surprised. Tyler would prefer certainty, but I reminded him nothing in life is certain." She grins. "What about you? Are you sticking around in LA?"

"It's as good a home base as any," I say, shrugging. "I have the cash to get my own place and leave Beck alone."

Between Ibiza, royalties, and more recent gigs, actual money is starting to pile up in my accounts.

"Beck says he never sees you."

I cut her a look. "Harrison and I are dating. It's getting serious."

"You think? The man wouldn't switch his breakfast cereal without a motive."

I round on her. "I didn't plan on this. He found out something that happened in my past, and I was so sure it would be the end, but it only made us closer."

"What?"

I haven't told anyone about this in years, but since the wedding, something in my chest has come loose, and I'm processing all these feelings. So, I fill my former roommate in on what happened with Zach, how I tried to bury it.

Her eyes shine with compassion, but she only puts a hand on my arm.

"If Harrison's the reason you're opening up about this, I'm glad."

"He's the reason for a lot of things," I admit, thinking of last night and how it felt to let loose with him.

"Such as?"

"He makes me coffee," I say bluntly.

Annie cocks her head. "And that's bad?"

"He used to drink this terrible fucking coffee. Until I bought a better kind. And a French press. The first night I stayed over, he made it for me. The man has never cooked a day in his life, never so much as made his own tea. But he makes me coffee every day."

"That's really sweet."

"This morning, I woke up, and my first thought

wasn't about the gig tonight or even seeing you. It was that I didn't have a cup of coffee to drink knowing that he'd made it with his own damn hands."

My exhale is heavy. "It's like the more real I am, the more he gets me."

"It's awesome?"

"It's fucking terrifying."

"I know what it's like to have someone see you, Rae. And I wish I could tell you that fear goes away, but it just changes. Hell, we're married, but there are still moments I'm terrified to lose Tyler. Not because I don't believe in him, but because I don't believe in me. Or I don't believe we deserve everything we have. There's only one thing I know for sure."

"What's that?"

"You're a performer. Whatever you feel, use it."

When I get ready for my show that night, I pick out a low-cut black top and tight pants with killer boots. Then I flip through my wigs, holding up one after another in the mirror.

None match my mood.

I stare at my reflection. Dark liner, top and bottom, frames my eyes. Thick eyelashes. A tube of plum lipstick waits on the dresser.

I reach for a lip balm instead. My lips are dry from chewing on them.

Little Queen is me, and she isn't. At the time, I thought I created her because I wanted a place to feel free and safe to experiment.

But lately, I've been forced to step outside my comfort zone without that protection. And I've survived.

They want how you make them feel. But more than that, they want who you are.

I ignore the wigs and tug the elastic out of my own hair, scrunching it so it falls around my head.

If tonight is my last chance at getting to Wild Fest, I'm going to give them a show.

I'll give them me.

21

HARRISON

From the second I landed in London, the city that should've felt like home, I've wanted to get back to Rae. The posh flat I've spent hundreds of nights in felt empty without her next to me.

"I did what you asked," my finance lead informed me from across the table in our London offices. "I have the bridge financing so you can increase your bid for La Mer. And we tripped up a new deal of Mischa's to make it harder for him. But there's a problem. He caught one of our men looking around after hours on one of his new projects. Apparently, faced with the prospect of losing something of value to him, the man talked. Which means he knows you're behind it."

I need to finalize the La Mer deal. And quickly.

That wasn't the only bad news.

My investigator informed me he discovered records of a seven-figure payment more than a decade ago—not *to* my parents, but *from* them. His hypothesis was it was an investment in the expansion of the Ivanov empire.

"They must have brokered a deal as part of their exit," I told him.

"Except other stakeholders in the organization made the same payment. People who are working there to this day."

I didn't have an explanation for that, as much as I wanted to.

The words haunted me all the way back to LA.

My parents weren't criminals. It's impossible.

They were decent people. Everything I've done is for them—the business I've built, the Ibiza club I've done everything to claim.

Not everything, a voice says.

I had a chance at it earlier in the summer.

My future in exchange for the club.

In some ways, I've already pledged it. But it felt different pledging myself to Christian's daughter.

At least, it did once Raegan Madani barged into my life.

We haven't talked much in the past forty-eight hours thanks to work and traveling. But when she called me from New York after I finished packing, the night turned into one I won't soon forget.

Her touching herself, letting me watch, fucking *getting off* on me watching...

It was the hottest thing I've ever seen.

I need to touch her. I've been rubbing myself raw since that night.

It's not only her body I miss, it's the snippy comments, the way she goes into a trance when she's working hunched over her computer, the little sigh of contentedness when I pull her against me in the morning and she's still asleep.

She's scheduled to get back to LA today, too, and I have plans for her.

Unknown: Thought you'd be interested in this.

The text that comes in when I land at LAX comes with a photo. It's taken from a distance, but the men in it are clearly visible. One in particular is familiar, and he's the one that counts.

I head to my condo to shower and change—shirt only, no jacket.

On impulse, I grab some of the books I brought to LA as reminders of home, a few from my father's collection and ones I've acquired since, and pack them into a bag I take down to my car.

On the way to the club, I text Rae to remind her I'm picking her up for dinner and she's not leaving my bed for a week.

As I enter the warehouse, the gazes of the workmen flick toward me, then away.

Leni looks up from her phone on the couch of the office. "Your girlfriend is hot. Did you see the posts?"

I grab the phone out of her hands to find a video of Rae mixing. Not Little Queen, either, but *my* Raegan. She's a goddess with straight dark hair, dark clothes, rimmed eyes that blaze with enough intensity to steal a man's soul when she looks up.

She's moving to the music. The crowd is in it with her. The headphones I bought her are around her neck, and I have a brief fantasy of locking them there to hold her in place while I fuck her until we're both sweaty and sore.

I want it, but I also want the moments after,

when I'd hold her so tight her breath fans my skin and her heart beats against mine.

"You're in love with her, aren't you?"

The words have my gaze snapping to Leni's. I could argue, but there's as much sense lying to one of my best friends as there is lying to myself.

"Do you wish I wasn't?"

"I like her, Harry, and I'm glad she makes you happy. But I remember what happened last time."

"Raegan is twice the woman Eva was."

"I know. I just don't want it to mess with your head, or your business." Leni grabs the phone back. "No more until we get this figured out," she chastises.

I arch a brow as I set the bag of books on the desk. "This being...?"

"It's been three days and there's nothing on the zoning approval since the hearing." Her frown deepens. "The audio equipment is arriving any moment."

I think back to my confrontation with Whelan, and the consequences of it.

She's not holding any sharp objects—I do a quick scan to make sure.

"There's going to be a delay in the planning

department. The head of zoning has been arrested."

I unzip the bag, carefully remove two of the books, and take them to the shelf opposite.

"Arrested? For what?"

Pleased with how they look, I go back for two more.

"There are already steps underway to mitigate the inevitable delay this will cause in zoning approvals," I go on. "So, I need you to pay a visit to the deputy director before this breaks. The committee reports have been filed. Explain that Whelan signed off verbally and promised to rubber-stamp it for us today. If he balks, remind him of the revenue projections and tax implications. If he stalls or says he needs to discuss with Whelan, convince him that would be unwise."

"And it would be unwise because...?"

I retrieve the last of the books, including the plastic-protected second edition Dumas that Rae pulled off my shelf in Ibiza, nearly dropping once she realized its age and value.

"Because Whelan's not returning to work. Today or ever."

I arrange the books on the shelf and step back to admire my work. There's still too much room on the other shelves below. If I'm going to be sticking around awhile, I need to add more books, or perhaps a sculpture.

Leni steps between me and the shelf, her eyes wide with horror. "Harrison, what the fuck have you—"

"Time to celebrate?"

The low, feminine voice from the doorway has me turning, though Leni doesn't release her grip on my arms.

My girlfriend stands in the office doorway, holding a bottle of champagne. She's wearing the dress I bought her and had delivered to Beck's. It's black and strapless, hugging her curves. As she reaches up to pull the sunglasses from her hair and set them and her phone on the desk, her cuff glints gold in the overhead lights. She looks healthy and happy and *mine*.

It's been three days since I've been inside her, and I'm about to die from the injustice of it all.

Leni crosses to Rae and takes the champagne bottle. "That's the good shit. What's the occasion?"

"I booked Wild Fest. Just got the email this afternoon. More than that… the stream from my show racked up a million views in two days. I have offers coming in from everywhere." Her slow smile is dazed and my chest aches with pride.

"Good for you," Leni comments. "I wish we had as much to celebrate, but—"

"Leni, could you find us glasses?" I cut her off smoothly.

I don't want news of Whelan's arrest taking away from Raegan's day, her triumph.

Thankfully, Rae's oblivious. "It's fine. I figured we'd pass it around."

I take the bottle and unwrap it, then open it with a pop.

Leni takes a long swig before passing it back to Rae. "Well, it's not a zoning permit"—my friend gives me side-eye—"but it's something. Excuse me while I get back to work."

As Leni heads out to the warehouse, I round the desk to Rae.

Waves of dark hair fall around her shoulders in a way that should be haphazard but only makes me want to fist it while I fuck her.

When she takes a drink from the bottle, my attention locks on her lips. I want to kiss her mouth.

I want to own it.

Rae offers me the bottle, and every part of me

tightens, including my grip on the neck of the champagne.

"Congratulations. Your show was incredible," I murmur. "I watched every clip I could find. Eventually I stopped because there wasn't a newspaper large enough to cover the tent in my trousers when I got off the plane."

She laughs. "Chartered flights, the official sponsor of dirty old men everywhere."

"It wasn't only a great performance, Raegan. It was you."

I'm in love with her. But I can't say it now, not with everything going on.

The expensive fabric of her dress is thin, but it feels too thick under my thumbs where they stroke her sides. I drag her farther into the office and kick the door shut.

"Can't take this," I mutter when I press her back to the door. Her lips are champagne and possibility, and I'm giddy on the taste of her. "You're dressed head to toe in things I got you. It's fucking hot."

My fingers find the zipper at her back.

"So why're you in a hurry to get them off?" Her voice is breathless.

"Because what's underneath is mine too." I

unzip the dress and push it off her. If I had the upper hand, it's gone when she straightens from laying the dress over my desk and I take in her lingerie-clad body.

Her golden skin peeks through the black lace of the bra, the triangle at the tops of her thighs.

"I see you did some shopping yourself."

She shrugs. "I was in New York."

I skim the curve of her breast, the lace and her heaviness beneath making my throat dry. "I approve."

"Well thank fuck, because I was waiting for that." Her sassy comeback makes me grin.

"These curves are soft," I murmur. "Inside, you've got edges."

"I'll take that as a compliment."

"Take everything I say as a compliment."

Her eyes shine as she presses up to kiss me. "Even when I'm stubborn?"

"Perfect," I groan when she tugs on my hair.

"A hermit?"

"It's cute."

"Sleep until noon?"

"Means I get to watch you dream."

I drag her harder against me, loving her gasp as the best parts of us collide.

"I used to think you were this beautiful, untouchable asshole," she murmurs. "But you're just a man."

"I wish I was a better one." I search her face, memorizing every line and curve. "I've done things I'm not proud of, for good reasons and bad ones. My sins can't be erased."

"I like you best when you're not perfect. When you can be yourself with me, because it means I can be myself with you."

Fuck.

She wants the unvarnished version of Harrison King.

I've never shown it to anyone. Not the way I have with her.

I reach for the button on my pants, and she lifts her chin, lips parting in anticipation.

She takes a long drink of champagne, for fun or courage, then holds it out. "You don't want any?"

I shake my head. "That's your reward. You're mine."

22

RAE

When I got the official word that I won the fan vote spot at Wild Fest, I had a mini meltdown. I'm not a girl who's used to getting what she wants. The fact that I had to work my ass off for it only made it sweeter.

Harrison King, on the other hand, knows exactly how to get what he wants.

From the second I walked in and spotted him, his gorgeous face tight and his expression intent, it was clear he wanted me.

He shifts me up onto the desk, stepping between my thighs and squeezing my ass.

My pulse races. There's a fine line between thrill and danger, one made sharper by the look in his eyes.

The man might actually be an animal.

He cups my breast in one large hand, the coarseness through the lace I wore for him feeling so damn good. I'm suddenly aware of tradespeople working outside.

"Is this room soundproof?"

Harrison's grin is wicked as he shrugs out of his jacket and strips off his shirt. "You have a problem with anyone hearing you, you're going to have to stay quiet."

My attention drags to his beautiful body, all angles and ripples of muscle. If I did have a problem, he'd stop. But I've already faced down one fear. This is a celebration of that, a way to show myself I can take more.

Until he shifts closer, rubbing his impressive erection against me through the lace and the fabric of his pants. He takes my other breast too, his fingers and thumbs rolling my nipples, and my head falls back.

"Oh, shit." The words spilling from my lips only make him twist harder. Heat drags a line from my breasts to my core, where I'm already wet.

"Beautiful girl." It's a praise and a taunt at once, and when his lips claim mine, I moan into his mouth. Most of the time, the difference in our ages and experience falls away when we're together. But once in awhile, he reminds me.

Like the commanding way he says, "Lie down."

Harrison reaches for the champagne, holding it over my reclined body. My stomach tightens as he tips it over and...

I hiss out a breath as it hits my breast, cold on my already peaked nipple. His mouth is there the next second, sucking roughly through the damp lace in a way that makes my thighs shake.

"The desk—"

"Christening it, and you."

"Like a boat?" I taunt. "You hate boats."

He retaliates by dropping fizzing champagne in my belly button and sucking it up. It tickles and thrills at once, and my legs wrap around his hips on instinct.

Next between my legs. The cold makes me jerk, but his hot mouth is there to lick it up.

When he drags off his pants and black boxer briefs, he steps back. "You trust me?"

"Yes."

He pins my wrists over my head and my body tenses instinctively at the feeling of being restrained and helpless. But the look on his face tells me I'm safe with him, that he'd take on the world for me.

"I don't take that for granted one goddamned second, Raegan."

My heart skips a beat.

He yanks my thong to the side, sinking two fingers inside my wet core.

The grip on my wrist doesn't relent. After a few pumps of his fingers that build the ache inside me, I'm grateful he's holding me down. Otherwise, I might float off into space.

"You're beautiful, and you're mine," he rasps, bending close to run his lips along my neck, my jaw. "Today. Tomorrow. No matter what. Tell me you want that."

His thumb presses down on my clit, fingers still playing with me, and I explode under his hands.

"Yes. *Fuck*, yes."

Harrison soaks up every second of my reaction with blazing eyes and tight body.

"How is it possible that every time we finish, I want more?" I pant.

"You saying you're not satisfied?" We both know he's joking, because I've probably had more orgasms since meeting him than I had in my life before.

"I'm saying you're turning me into a monster."

He strokes down my cheek, eyes softening. "We'll be monsters together, love."

He's dragging my thighs apart to shift between them when my phone goes off on the desk near my head.

"Ignore it," he growls, playing with me as he strokes his hard length, preparing to fuck me.

I do, but it rings again a moment later.

Frustration fills me and I grab for the phone, meaning to switch it to silent, but when I see the name I suck in a breath.

"I have to get this."

"Don't."

There's an edge to his quick response that's more than irritation, but I push on Harrison's bare chest until he lets me up.

"It's my brother."

"What happened to the honeymoon?" I ask Kian when he shows me to a private office at the end of the long hallway of his medical practice.

I haven't been here since he opened it more than five years ago. The standalone building is shiny and new looking, with a cheery yellow waiting room and a perky receptionist.

"I had to wrap up some things here before we left, so I planned a week in between." He reaches into the bar fridge and pulls out a water, holding it up. I shake my head, and he opens it, taking a long drink.

"My wife told me you gave us a very generous gift," he goes on, though the small talk feels awkward. "You're my little sister. You didn't need to do that."

"It was my pleasure." I recall the check I dashed out and stuck in a card. "So, do you want to tell me what you didn't want to talk about over the phone?"

His brows knit together as he shifts a hip against the large desk holding a monitor, note-book computer, and reams of files. "I got a call from Zach. He's been arrested. Technically, it was a call from his lawyer, who wanted to talk to a few of his friends. Sounds like there are multiple charges. Sexual assault. Possession of pornography of underaged women. Girls," he amends.

The blood drains from my head.

The floor tilts under my feet, and I press a

hand to my stomach as if it'll stop the sudden lightheadedness.

"I just finished meeting with his lawyer, and your name came up."

He swallows once, again, as if forming words takes an unusual amount of energy. "Did something happen with Zach?"

"I'll take that water."

He listens while I explain what happened ten years ago. I expected it to be impossible, but I've told Harrison and Annie, and the practice seems to have made it easier.

"Raegan, I don't know what to say." He rubs both hands over his face.

"Mom and Dad didn't want to deal with it. I heard them arguing about it. Mom was pissed, but Dad said no one would take it seriously."

"I didn't know what the problem was, but I saw the guilt eat at them whenever I visited," he admits.

"How close are you and Zach?"

Kian straightens, his face a mask of agony and disbelief. "He stood up for me, but now... I don't know how I'll look him in the eye again."

"Dr. Madani?" The receptionist is at the door,

looking apologetic. "I'm sorry, but you wanted me to keep you on schedule."

"I'll be right there." He nods, and she looks between us before walking back down the hall. "What do you need from me, Rae?"

"You didn't have my back then. Have it now."

The emotions swirling in me as I leave are less about what happened then and more about processing the news that Zach's been arrested.

There's no way Zachary Whelan went from a career to a future in a jail cell, or that he did something that got him caught in the last few days after a decade. I don't believe in coincidence when Harrison King is concerned.

It was Harrison. It must have been. He's the only thing that's changed in this equation.

Was he waiting for updates while we were fucking in his office? What about in New York, the night before my show? Had he already put this in motion?

When I head over to Harrison's place, I'm remembering how he said we aren't like normal people. The reminder of how easily he can wield that power and for whatever he wants hits me like a bucket of ice.

23

HARRISON

*a*s I pull up to the building, my phone rings with a number from Spain.

"Christian," I say when I answer. "What a pleasant surprise. We're not due to talk for another three days."

I toss my keys to the valet as Christian's cough comes over the line. "I'm afraid it can't wait."

I stride through the door held by the doorman and straight into my elevator.

"I'm selling La Mer to Mischa."

My grip tightens on the phone. "What did he offer? I'll match it," I go on as the elevator reaches the top floor and the bell dings.

"It's not a price you can match." His voice wavers. "It's over, Harrison."

I force myself out into my penthouse condo, standing in the middle of the entryway in front of the mirror.

The luxe backdrop blurs. Nothing matters except the man on the other end of the phone.

"You wanted me to investigate my parents as a way to bide time and run up Mischa's bid."

"No. I wanted to give you the chance to prove your parents weren't duplicitous."

I don't believe him. "From the moment I rejected your offer of La Mer in exchange for marrying your daughter, you weren't intending to sell to me."

I pace the hall, my voice rising.

"This isn't about honor, Christian. It's about money and pride." My laugh is humourless. "You and Ivanov deserve one another."

There's a beat of silence, then a second, before he clicks off.

I stare at the mirror.

Even if I was focused on the club here, it was all in service of winning La Mer. Now, I've lost the thing that mattered most.

I slam my fist into the glass.

Rae

I'm standing in the bathroom freshening up, waiting for Harrison to return and trying to deal with Whelan's arrest.

I need to know if he's behind it. If he is, I'm not sure how to feel. On one hand, I'm grateful Whelan is being forced to account for his crime— crimes, if what Kian says is true.

But having my business handled so neatly by another person leaves me feeling a different kind of exposed.

The sound of the door jerks me out of my thoughts.

Harrison's speaking to someone on the phone.

"...wanted me to investigate my parents as a way to bide time and run up Mischa's bid."

He's speaking with Christian.

I'm about to make my presence known when Harrison's angry voice comes down the hall.

"From the moment I rejected your offer of La Mer in exchange for marrying your daughter, you weren't intending to sell to me."

What the fuck?

His next words are drowned out by the buzzing in my ears.

Christian wanted Harrison to marry his daughter? The woman he showed around town? That's what Leni was talking about him sacrificing for me.

The sound of breaking glass jars me out of my thoughts.

I trip down the hall to the entry and living room.

"Harrison!"

He's not here.

Fear rises up my throat.

A scraping noise from the huge deck has my head snapping around. I run to the glass door and drag it open.

Harrison is the stiffest person ever to grace a lounge chair. He stares out over the skyline, no jacket, sleeves rolled up.

His hands fall to his sides. That's when I see the white kitchen towel wrapped around his knuckles, the rusty stains seeping through.

"Shit, Harrison! What happened?"

I drop to my knees at his side.

"Christian sold La Mer to Mischa." The words are low and brittle. "I've been trying to find evidence to exonerate my parents—in London and before. But it was all a ruse to run up Mischa's bid. It's over. Everything I've fought for the past decade is gone."

His agony shreds me. I've seen him furious, controlling. I've seen him caring, wanting. I've never seen him broken.

"But why would Christian give you all this time to prove yourself, then go back on his word at the last minute?"

"I offended his pride."

I shift over his lap, straddling him. "Does this have to do with turning down his offer of La Mer in exchange for marrying his daughter?"

Surprise flares in his eyes that I know. "Yes."

"That's fucked up," I breathe.

"His offer or the fact that I declined it?"

"Both." What kind of twisted shit is it that a man would trade his daughter for a property? I think of meeting Christian, how devoted he seemed to his family. "If he made you the offer, he must have thought you'd accept it. So why didn't you?"

Harrison angles his head back against the lounger, looking at me through half-lidded eyes. "You know why."

I run my hands over Harrison's jaw, the unshaven shadow rough against my thumbs.

"Whelan was arrested today," I say. "Tell me you had nothing to do with it."

His eyes go flat. "He raped you."

"I know, I was there," I retort. "Did you know about his arrest when I came to see you at the club earlier?"

His nostrils flare, and I have my answer even without him speaking a word.

"I told you I'm not a perfect man. Sometimes I'm not even a good one. You said you liked that about me."

"I like that we're both imperfect and we can figure things out together," I argue. "Not that you snap your fingers and make decisions regular people don't get to make."

He shoves out from under me and I nearly fall onto the concrete patio.

"There was no question about turning down Christian's offer last summer, just as there was no question about sending Whelan to prison."

He stalks to the end of the balcony.

"Because you always make the right decisions?" I shout after him.

He turns, the towel falling off his bleeding hand. "Because I fucking love you!" he roars.

Shock reverberates through my body.

He stares down at me, daring me to argue with him.

Harrison King loves me.

This man who buys and sells property, travels the world, pursues vendettas and does it all in a custom suit to hide behind the pain he's endured and the enormous pressure he's put on himself, loves me.

I cross to him and pick up the towel. Reaching for his hand, I wrap the clean side of the fabric around his knuckles again.

"I'm glad you didn't get La Mer from Christian," I say. "Because then I wouldn't have you." My hand slips between the buttons of his shirt, my fingers grazing the scar I know by memory. "People can mark us, but they can't define us. We can move on and live again and trust again." *You taught me that.* "What did Mischa win, really? A pile of concrete built by another man? You've taken a warehouse and dreamed it into a place people can be free and feel alive. It's going to be spectacular. You can make your own legacy as someone who creates, not merely conquers. Tell me you want that."

Because if he does, he'll find a way to get it. This man I fell for without wanting to.

His chest heaves, his beautiful blue eyes clouded with pain of his own. He reaches down with his good hand to brush a tear I never noticed from my face.

"I want to want it."

The cuff on my wrist catches the light, and when he lifts my hand and presses his lips to my wrist right below the bracelet he bought to tell me he wasn't leaving, I feel a glimmer of hope for him.

Hope for us.

24

RAE

"*S*hit. We're supposed to bring a gift," I call as I fasten my earrings in front of the powder room mirror.

"Only if you want to be invited back."

"It's Tyler and Annie's housewarming. They're not going to un-friend us, right? And he's already been living there for ages."

I duck into the hall to see Harrison stepping into his shoes at the front door. He looks breathtakingly sexy in dark trousers and a button-down shirt. No jacket.

It's a win.

The past two weeks have been a struggle, but we're moving forward. I can tell he's having a difficult time, but he always finds a smile when

I'm around. I wish he didn't try so hard for my sake.

One piece of good news is that Zachary Whelan is in jail and was denied bail. But thanks to the delays in the planning department, some of the most important renovations at the new club are on hold. It's eating at Harrison.

"I have a gift for you," I inform him as we step into the elevator and hit the button for the ground floor.

I hold out the notification on my phone.

"The zoning was approved?"

"This morning," I confirm.

Disbelief fills his handsome face. "How the hell did you get that before I did?"

"Leni."

"Fuck."

He crosses to me as the doors open, taking my face between his palms.

He kisses me, long and deep, before coming up for air.

"I need to check on the club on the way. Make sure everyone's on the job working twice as fast."

"No, you don't," I say quickly, and he grimaces.

"I'll pull up the security footage. Just to make sure everything on the exterior is on schedule."

As we exit the elevators at the lobby, he reaches for his phone.

I try to bat it away. "Don't you trust Leni?"

His frown is exasperated. "I did until she booked me to give that presentation yesterday to a group of LA entrepreneurs without telling me. It was out of character."

It's also why I've been working on something special the past few days, something that requires him to be far away from the club in order for it to be a surprise.

In the end, he's too strong and I can't get his phone.

He stops in the middle of the lobby, pulling up the security footage.

Shit. I squeeze my eyes shut...

"The fuck is wrong with the security cameras?" he gripes.

I exhale and peer around his arm at the screen. "It looks like the interior one is fine. Just the street view is shorted out."

Thank you, Leni, I say in my head.

I lay a hand on his cheek, brushing my thumb along his jaw. "We should stop and pick up a gift though."

"No, we shouldn't." He takes my hand, nodding

to the doorman as we pass out into the sunshine and approach Harrison's car that the valet has pulled up.

"Yeah, we should. Annie's pregnant, and you're supposed to buy shit for babies, right?"

"Their gift is already being delivered." Harrison rounds to the driver's side.

I pull up, staring at him. Of course he ordered a gift and had it delivered. It's probably something thoughtful and expensive, and he knows I suck at friend-ing and didn't even point it out.

"I love you."

He freezes before turning back. "Say it again."

"I love you."

He comes back to me and kisses me against the side of the car until I'm breathless.

Fuck breathing. It's overrated. Especially when the alternative is having Harrison King's possessive mouth worshipping mine.

"We're going back inside," he murmurs.

"No time," I pant in response.

"Wasn't asking."

Harrison

Eventually we make it to Tyler and Annie's place in the Hills. Apparently, Tyler rented the house last year while he was finishing his album and just bought it. It's stunning, modern and white with a pool facing the view over West Hollywood.

Most of the couple dozen people at the party are familiar. Annie's father, Jax Jamieson, semi-retired yet still fully the most famous rock star in the world, along with his wife and their two young children. Rae's friends Beck and Elle.

"The ice sculpture is beautiful," Annie says, half-serious and half-amused as she surveys the giant form now occupying their table.

Rae snorts and turns to me. "Isn't that what you sent them for their New York housewarming?"

"It is. It's why we also sent something else. Because it'll melt faster here."

Her laugh bubbles up from somewhere deep inside, and fuck if I don't love that sound more every time I hear it.

Annie tugs Rae away to talk with Annie's step-mother, Haley, and I head out to the patio with Tyler and Beck. I can't help admiring at the view—

not of the ocean, but back at the house. The family and friends all around.

There's love here. The kind I've missed since my parents died and the kind I hadn't let myself hope for since long before Eva.

"Who's your realtor?" I hear myself asking.

Tyler turns toward me, looking surprised. "I thought your penthouse had three bedrooms."

I shrug as I lift my glass to my lips. "A man always wants more."

He and Beck exchange a look before Tyler shakes his head.

"Does Rae know about this?" he asks.

"I find it's best to work out the details, then start working on her."

They grin.

"Damn," Beck says. "She's got you."

I cut a look over my shoulder to see Rae inside with the other women. I love her, and the way she told me she loved me too today... it was everything.

I've been thinking about what I'd do if besting Mischa wasn't my only goal. Ceding La Mer always felt like a failure, but I've never considered what I'd gain. I could experiment with complementary business lines that interest me. Perhaps smaller venues in new markets. Partnerships with the local community.

Echo Entertainment could slow down and look the fuck around, and so could I.

"Harrison King, family man. Whatever would the tabloids say?" Beck says, smirking.

"He's not a family man yet," Tyler comments. "Did you see the announcement for the new club?"

"*Kings*," Beck chortles. "You've been in the States too long, friend. Whatever British tendency to understatement you had is gone."

Beck pulls up the social post on his phone—the one that went public through dozens of influencers who've committed to opening night, plus my company, scores of media outlets, and, of course, Little Queen.

"Everyone in the world will be watching you," Beck notes.

I cast a look at Rae talking with the other women. "Fucking let them."

We toast.

"You guys seem good," Annie says over her non-alcoholic cocktail as we sit around the couch. The living room looks out on the patio and pool and West Holly-wood beyond.

"We're figuring it out," I admit.

"You sure looked like you had it figured out at Spago last week." She holds out her phone with a gossip column picture of me and Harrison after our meal at the restaurant.

"Since when do you comb the gossip online?"

"Since they started posting pictures of my favorite private couple. What was he saying to you?"

My hand is laced in his, and he's whispering in my ear.

"Don't remember." I blink back at my friend.

"Bullshit."

She's right. I totally remember.

Annie's six-year-old half sister, Sophie, climbs up next to me with a book in hand.

"You want me to read?" I ask her, amused.

"No. I'll read to you."

She starts to, and I tuck back the soft hair that falls over her face.

"Watch out, or you'll have some of your own soon," Elle jokes, dropping onto the chair across from us.

My usual knee-jerk shudder isn't there.

"Not soon," I correct. "Maybe someday."

Annie leans in, hopeful. "Do you love him?"

I sneak a look at Harrison.

"You do," she goes on without my answering.

"It's almost like the harder it gets, the closer we are. If that makes sense."

She nods, enthusiastic.

My phone buzzes with text from Leni, along with a picture.

Excitement jolts through me. "Oh my God. No way."

"What?" Elle demands.

I explain what I've been working on, and Annie sighs.

"Send me a picture of his face when you show him."

Elle nudges her with a toe. "A, His face is going to be eating her once she shows him."

Annie claps hands over Sophie's ears, glaring at us both.

Like it's my fault my boyfriend is a billionaire with a magic fucking tongue.

The rest of the afternoon is fun, and it's almost twilight by the time we leave.

"You're right," I say as Harrison navigates the roads from the Hills. "We should stop at the club."

He cuts me a surprised look. "Since when?"

I lift a shoulder. "Since now."

He reaches over to take my hand in his.

When we turn onto the street, the sun setting behind us and leaving long shadows from trees and buildings, Harrison starts to tense.

High in the air, lights beckon, growing brighter with every second.

"What the...?"

My breath hitches. "We're not even in the parking lot," I prod.

He ignores me and parks the car on the street, shifting out to stare up at the marquee on the side of the building.

Kings.

It's lit up in orange and gold, shaped like a crown. It reminds me of the Ibiza summer or a Phoenix rising.

I round the car and lean against his side. "Everyone who sees this will know it's yours. We wanted to surprise you. Okay, I wanted to surprise you," I amend. "Leni helped."

How we see ourselves is important. How Harrison sees this place is important.

He grabs me and pulls me against his hard chest. His heart hammers through the clothing that separates us, but it's his expression of awe that humbles me.

"You're unbelievable," he murmurs against my hair. "When you said I could put Ivanov in the past, I didn't believe you. But now, seeing this place, it feels possible."

"You don't need to protect your parents' legacy anymore. You can have your own."

His arms are an iron grip around me.

It's three in the morning, and I'm awake.

Not because I'm stressed or anxious. Because I'm *happy*.

We're lying in bed together, Harrison asleep while I replay the moment he saw the sign I ordered over and over, when the phone vibrates on his side of the bed.

He stirs, groaning before he reaches for it to answer.

The moment he does, his gorgeous body tightens, and he shoots to sitting.

"Since when?"

He curses, and alarm bolts through me. I grab for his arm, but he's already halfway out of bed and still on the phone.

"What is it?" I demand.

Harrison hits the lights by the door before moving to the dresser to grab clothing. He drags on sweatpants, still listening.

"What's wrong?" I repeat, shifting out of bed after him.

He hangs up and riffles through his drawer. "Leni got a notification the security cameras are down at Kings."

"We turned off the exterior ones this week so

the sign would be a surprise." I grab him a long-sleeved T-shirt and hold it out. He tugs it on with a grateful look.

"There was a problem rebooting them, and now all the cameras are down. We have no video of the premises."

A chill runs through me. "Can't someone else deal with it?" It's late, and this is why he has people who work for him.

"I have a bad feeling."

I follow him to the door. "I'll come with you."

The look he shoots me is quelling. "No. Stay here. I'll call you if something's wrong."

That stalls me enough that I let him go. I stand numbly in the foyer.

I can't reconcile our day with the middle-of-the-night call.

My feet carry me down the hall toward the bedroom.

It occurs to me how different this is from the last time I found myself alone in Harrison King's room in the morning without him nearby. In Ibiza, I was afraid he didn't have feelings, that everything that had gone down between us was a lie or a flirtation.

There's none of that fear now. He loves me.

The bedroom feels disrupted, the covers on the bed thrown back. Hastily opened drawers stare back at me.

I won't wait for him, I decide. I'm going after him.

I pull on jeans and a sweater, not bothering with a bra or brushing my hair. I snap on my gold cuff like a security measure before heading for the elevator.

The concierge looks worried when I demand a car, but he relents, waving over the valet to pull around a Nissan that evidently belongs to the concierge.

I jump in and navigate to the club. Even at three thirty in the morning, the drive is half an hour.

When I get there, the first thing I see are the flames. I hear sirens and see the lights of the approaching fire truck. They cut me off before I can turn off the road. I follow them in, my heart dropping through my stomach as I take in the sight before me.

The club is on fire.

Acrid black smoke pours out of broken windows. The sign isn't lit, or the bulbs have shattered from the heat. The building is concrete, but the inside is wood.

Worse, Harrison's car is in the lot, angled awkwardly with the driver's door open.

There's no sign of Harrison.

The sound of tires screeching in behind me has me whirling to find Leni, who I recall lives twice as far from the club as Harrison.

"Where is he?" she hollers, wide-eyed.

"I don't..." I turn back toward the building in horror.

Firefighters pour out of the fire truck, a couple of them uncoiling the long hose from the vehicle's side.

I start for the building and make it to within a dozen feet of the door before heat blasts open another window, glass flying outward. My hands fly up too late to shield myself, but the next second, Leni's there.

"We need to get you back," she says.

"But Harrison—he must be in there!"

I can't breathe, and it's not only because of the smoke.

I run to the firefighters. "You need to find him."

Before the firefighter can say anything, two others bring Harrison out of the club. He's stumbling between them, breathing through a mask, his arms clutched against his chest.

I'm over there in a heartbeat, and Harrison's pushing something into my hands before they usher him into an ambulance.

"You were with him."

I look up to see an officer blocking the hallway I've been pacing for the last two hours. It's been a long night at the hospital while Harrison has been put through a barrage of tests. I've heard almost nothing about his condition except that he's stable. The doctor told me that as if I should have been relieved—like the fact that the man I love running into his burning building had a happy ending after all.

"Who are you?" I demand.

The officer gives me his name. "I need to ask you a few questions. Let's find chairs and talk."

"I'm not going anywhere."

He sizes me up, his gaze landing on my bracelet. He nods toward the side of the hallway, and I grudgingly step out of the way of traffic.

"You were the first person on the scene."

"Second," I correct. "Harrison got there first."

The last time a police officer surveyed me so intently, I was a teenager at the front desk of the local branch, deciding whether to report what had happened to me. I was nervous, sweating. In the end, fear overtook me, and I turned around and never went back.

Not only fear of the police, but fear of being found out, exposed, judged, ridiculed, hated.

"How did it start?" I demand.

"It's too soon to say."

"Was it...? Tell me it wasn't the marquee." My voice fades to a whisper.

He relents. "I heard the firefighters say there was some kind of accelerant inside. Now, Mr. King was found in the building. The *only* person found in the building."

Hostility slices through the fear in my gut. "You don't think he did this? Kings is set to open in less than three months."

"Why would he be inside?"

"To try and save his damned club!"

He sighs, and I play with the strap on my purse.

"We'll be reviewing security footage. If anyone

was staking out the building after dark this week, or arrived tonight, maybe we'll be able to see who."

No, you won't.

Thanks to me, the exterior security cameras have been out for the past two days.

26

HARRISON

"You need to lie down."

I look up from where I'm seated on the side of the hospital bed at the nurse's voice.

"I'm fine," I rasp, spreading my hands carefully to avoid jarring the IV in the back of one.

It's been hours since I got here. I have no idea how many as I've been subjected to countless tests and questions. My lungs burn from the smoke. I've been turning over what happened.

How I arrived at my new club to see it engulfed in flames.

I ran inside to see if I could find the root of the damage.

Raegan appears in the doorway, dressed in

clothes she must've pulled on in a hurry, her hair tugged up in a messy knot. Her face sags with relief when she sees me, before her brows pull together in concern.

"You're here." My words end on a cough. I grab water from the table, swallowing rapidly.

"I got to the club soon after you did." Rae brushes past the nurse to my side.

I crumple the paper cup in my grip. "I told you to stay at the condo."

The words are harsh, but she doesn't flinch.

"I'm supposed to watch the man I love walk away? I don't think so." Her lips twitch. "Besides, you're not as scary as you think you are."

I glance down to take in the hospital gown. "Christ."

"They were out of Brioni."

My eyes narrow, but her fingers thread with mine, making the IV tug. It's nothing compared to the pain to come.

"They said it wasn't the sign," she whispers, and if it's possible, I feel worse at her expression of guilt.

"It wasn't the sign," I tell her firmly. The beautiful sign she arranged to have put up while I was distracted.

Unfortunately, that distraction had a price.

"But there's no surveillance footage of any vehicles in the area, anyone who could've shown up to set the fire. They said they'll canvass other businesses in the area to look for clues."

"They won't find anything." My words are biting, and she flinches.

"Why not?"

"Because Mischa did this."

Raegan's dark eyes blink. "He has La Mer."

"It's not enough."

Tonight, I realized how serious Mischa is.

This is more than business. It's personal.

He won't rest as long as I'm succeeding. As long as there's a chance for my happiness.

She grabs a visitor's chair and drags it to my bedside, perching on the edge. Reaching into her bag, she pulls out the book in its protective casing and hands it to me.

"They're still going through the building," she murmurs as I turn *The Count of Monte Cristo* in my hands. I managed to get to the office and retrieve it before the fire reached that part of the building. Thanks to its plastic casing, the book is relatively intact. "Leni's figuring out how much can be salvaged, but I've never been so glad it's a concrete brick. The bones are there, and the insurance should pay for the rest."

The businessman in my brain says even if it does, we're now months behind. We'll be burning cash, possibly at unsustainable rates.

"None of that is the problem," I say as I set the book in my lap. "*He* is."

The object of my vendetta, the one I was ready to set aside so I could have a life with the woman in front of me. He won't let me set it aside.

Which means I have no hope of building the future I want, the one Raegan deserves, without stopping him.

"I have to leave LA."

"Is your insurance in London?" She frowns. "I'm sure they can deal with it from here—"

"It's not about insurance."

Her elbow leans on the edge of my bed, and I get a hit of her familiar scent. That, plus her closeness, send a pang of longing through me.

"Okay. I have some shows lined up, but I'll cancel them if I need to." She pulls out her phone. "As long as we need to get this figured out..."

I push the phone away. "I can't take you with me."

The phone slips out of her hands as she realizes my intention. "What do you mean? You said you wanted to move on. There are other good things."

"Things like Kings?" I glance down at the book. "He burned it to the ground tonight."

She grabs my face in her hands, lifts my gaze to hers. "I've spent my life hiding from my past. I'm not hiding from my future." The cuff shines on her wrist. "I know it kills you that you can't control him—"

"This isn't a joke, isn't a game!" I'm shouting now, hoarsely. "This is real life."

"I know it is. That's why I'm not leaving."

I think of the news I got about my parents, that they weren't trying to escape the Ivanov's business but to reinvest in it.

I wanted to deny it, but tonight in the ambulance, I felt the tiniest flint spark deep in my chest. The part of me built for survival woke up for the first time in a long time, possibly since my parents died.

If they were something other than the saints I made them out to be, then part of me is, too.

"But I am," I say finally.

I was never meant to be a man who builds things...

I'm destined to be a man who destroys them.

I'm no better than Mischa Ivanov, only different.

Raegan's lips part in disbelief. Her eyes work over mine, emotion spilling over, but beneath, she's resolute. "In Denver, you gave me this, and you told me it meant you'd never go." She reaches for the bracelet on her wrist, waiting for me to tell her I meant it. That I love her, and that our love matters more than anything else in this world.

"I was wrong."

The words rip from my chest, and saying them is itself an act of destruction.

I see it on her face, in the way her shoulders tighten.

I'm hurting her. The person I love most is sitting in front of me and I'm destroying her.

The pain in my chest is so sharp, so sudden, I wonder if this is what a heart attack feels like.

Fucking stop this, a voice demands. But I close it in an iron fist.

Something lands on the bed next to me. With a last look, Raegan rises from her chair and speaks to the nurse before starting down the hall.

I can't breathe again, but there's nothing the machines can do for me.

My gaze lowers to the shimmering circle next to me on the bed.

The inscription stands in relief against the gold.

My Queen.

This is wrong. All wrong.

One at a time, I pry off the leads attached to my chest, tossing them aside. The machine they belong to emits a single beep of complaint. Next, I shove myself out of bed, the IV tugging itself from my hand.

"Mr. King!" the nurse says from the doorway, sounding alarmed. "You could aggravate your condition."

"You know nothing about my condition." I spit out the words as I stalk past her and down the hall, the tile cold on my bare feet.

I don't care that I'm wearing next to nothing. Don't give a shit what anyone sees. The wrongness in my gut drives me forward, past the burning in my lungs.

At the end of the hall, I'm breathing heavily.

But there's no sight of her.

27

RAE

*A*s I step off the plane in Ibiza, the wind catches my hair and whips it around my face.

"My bag?" I ask my driver, a kid who subtly checks me out as he holds the door.

"Already in your car, *señorita*. Forgive me. You're Raegan Madani, aren't you? The DJ Little Queen?"

I take off my sunglasses. "Sure am."

He leans in, his handsome face eager and so young. "You were ranked seventh on Billboard's Top 100 DJs list. No woman has ever been that high before."

"There'll be a lot more women that high soon."

I shift inside the car, and moments later, the driver pulls out.

En route, we drive past a familiar venue, my gaze lingering as my stomach heats.

"It's a famous club," the boy in the driver's seat boasts. "The biggest on the island. But you know that." He flushes.

"I've heard," I say, not unkindly.

The car winds up into the mountains before pulling up to the gates of the villa.

In the past eight months, through festivals and gigs from Sydney to Tokyo to Paris, my career has exploded in the best way.

I shift out of the car and start up the steps of the villa. The door opens before I can knock.

I expect to find a doorman, but I'm instantly accosted by a familiar face and body. One that has every muscle in me screaming.

"You're the last person I expected to see at the door of my villa."

If I thought Mischa Ivanov would look the same as I remembered, I was wrong. He's leaner, as if the past year has taken a toll on him.

Like a stray dog, he doesn't look weak. Only hungry.

"Then it's your lucky day."

His surprised eyes flash, cold in the Spanish heat surrounding us. "What would your lover say if he knew you were here?"

"Former," I correct, though I have no doubt he knows that. "And because he's former, I don't give a shit what Harrison would say."

I fold my arms behind my back, my thumb and forefinger lightly encircling the opposite wrist, pressing on the tattoo there.

Habit.

"Now is when you invite me in," I say.

He stares at me in disbelief, stunned the woman he hit wants to be invited into his home.

But I guess I've changed in the last year too.

I hold his gaze, unflinching.

Finally, he opens the door wider and motions with a jerk of his head.

I follow him.

Thank you for reading BEAUTIFUL SINS! I hope you loved diving deeper into Harrison and Rae's world.

Harrison and Rae's intense, addictive, emotional

story concludes with a bang in BEAUTIFUL RUIN!

SIGN UP FOR PIPER'S NEWSLETTER: www.piperlawsonbooks.com/subscribe

---

P.S.: By reading this story, you trusted me with your time and your heart. I will never take that trust for granted.

Harrison and Rae's story went to a darker place than some of my other books, but it felt necessary.

Sometimes, life takes us to that place. What happens *to* us doesn't matter—*cannot* matter—as much as who we choose to be in those moments, and the million moments after.

If you're feeling a little raw after this book, take comfort knowing we're in this together.

I promise Harrison and Rae will get everything they deserve.

This king and his queen have grown so much, and they'll need every ounce of the trust they've built to conquer one last challenge.

Beautiful Ruin drops August 11.

So bring your lucky headphones, grab a billionaire Brit or two, and get ready to flip your middle fingers in the air.

This is going to be one helluva show.

Love always,

Piper

THANK YOU

My readers are the most amazing readers anywhere. You guys are positive, bold, enthusiastic, supportive, and you inspire me daily.

If you enjoyed *Beautiful Sins*, I'd be beyond grateful if you could take two minutes to leave a quick review wherever you picked it up. Reviews are like gold to us authors.

If you do leave a review, I'd love to hear about it so I can thank you personally. Here're the best ways to reach out:
www.facebook.com/piperlawsonbooks
www.instagram.com/piperlawsonbooks
piper@piperlawsonbooks.com

Make sure you're on my VIP list to get updates, special giveaways and deals! Signup at: https://www.piperlawsonbooks.com/subscribe

Thanks for being awesome, for inspiring me, and for helping make it possible for me to do what I love.

xo,

Piper

BOOKS BY PIPER LAWSON

ENEMIES SERIES

Beautiful Enemy

Beautiful Sins

Beautiful Ruin

RIVALS SERIES

Love Notes

A Love Song for Liars

A Love Song for Rebels

A Love Song for Dreamers

A Love Song for Always

WICKED SERIES

Good Girl

Bad Girl

Wicked Girl

Forever Wicked

MODERN ROMANCE SERIES

Easy Love

Bad Love

Twisted Love

PLAY SERIES

<u>PLAY</u>

<u>NSFW</u>

RISE

TRAVESTY SERIES

<u>Schooled</u>

<u>Stripped</u>

<u>Sealed</u>

<u>Styled</u>

<u>Satisfaction</u>

ABOUT THE AUTHOR

Piper Lawson is a USA Today bestselling author of smart, steamy romance! She writes about women who follow their dreams (even the scary ones), best friends who know your dirty secrets (and love you anyway), and complex heroes you'll fall hard for (especially after talking with them). Brains or brawn? She'll never make you choose.

Piper lives in Canada with her tall, dark and brilliant husband. She believes peanut butter is a protein, rose gold is a neutral, and love is ALWAYS the answer.

I love hearing from you! Hang with me on:

The Interwebs➜www.piperlawsonbooks.com

Facebook➜www.facebook.com/piperlawsonbooks

Newsletter➜www.
piperlawsonbooks.com/subscribe

Instagram➜www.
instagram.com/piperlawsonbooks

Goodreads➜www.goodreads.com/author/
show/13680088

ACKNOWLEDGMENTS

This story wouldn't have happened without the support of my awesome readers, including my ARC team. You ladies provide endless enthusiasm, cheerleading, and help spreading the word. I could NOT do it without you, and it would be a lot less fun to try.

An extra shoutout to Suzanne, Anna and Beth for reading early! You guys are awesome.

Thank you Regina Wamba for the perfect image. This couple has been inspiring me for more than a year.

Becca Mysoor, thank you for your story genius.

Cassie Robertson and Devon Burke, thank you for questioning, polishing, and catching all the little things.

Thank you Dani Sanchez for your sage advice and for helping my stories find their way to the right readers.

And Annette Brignac and Michelle Clay... I would not be able to get these books to the people who matter most without you. Don't ever leave me.

Thank you all from the bottom of my heart. The best part of author life is having YOU in it.

Love always,

Piper

Made in the USA
Middletown, DE
28 November 2021

53614374R00175